A Chronicle of Magpies

STORIES

BRUCE MEYER

A Chronicle of Magpies

STORIES

BRUCE MEYER

TIGHTROPE BOOKS

Tightrope Books
2 College Street, Unit 206-207
Toronto, Ontario. M5G 1K3
www.tightropebooks.com

Copy editor: Deanna Janovski
Typesetter: Dawn Kresan
Cover design: Deanna Janovski
Author photo: Mark Raynes Roberts

We thank the Canada Council for the Arts and the Ontario
Arts Council for their support of our publishing program.

Library and Archives Canada Cataloguing in Publication

Meyer, Bruce, 1957–, author
A chronicle of magpies / Bruce Meyer.

Short stories. ISBN 978-1-926639-74-1 (pbk.)
        I. TITLE.

PS8576.E93C47 2014   C813'.54   C2014-903027-4

For Kerry, Katie, Margaret, and Carolyn

9   The First

19   The Watch

27   Boiling Point

29   A Chronicle of Magpies

85   States of Claude

105   The Dragon Cloth

123   Something Close to Brilliance,
       Something Close to Love

135   When in a Fine Day's Running

The First

"Grace! Give the spirtle a twirl. Can't you see the boy has lumps?" Hazel was serious about lumps. Grace stood over my bowl of oatmeal with the tiny wooden baseball bat that I had been playing with the night before and mashed the porridge against the side of the bowl. It did not improve the taste or the consistency. The congregation of elderly siblings seated at the long table in the tiny cottage lapped theirs up and looked around for more. I gagged. I was the last one still eating.

"Gobby, gobby," my grandfather said as his sisters stared at me in delighted admiration. The old man held out a spoonful from his own bowl for me to eat. He never put sugar on his porridge, and the thought of the beige meal going unsweetened into my mouth made my face red. There was so much suffering and history in that bowl. The oatmeal had sustained their lives and the lives of my ancestors for as long as time was a story. I was intended to eat the porridge. It was an honour. It was Scottish, and I was the first born grandson of the patriarch of the family, the "heir to the throne," as my grandfather always introduced me. What I was to inherit was not only their culture and their traditions, but the art of being a member of their family. I was the only child permitted to be among them at the gathering of the clan.

"I don't think he likes it," said Flora. I nodded my head in agreement.

Bea, who was too equatorial to sit at the table, filled an armchair in the corner and looked up. "You shouldn't have such a commotion about porridge. Your family has eaten it for generations." She raised her spoon coated in tiny globules to emphasize the point. "You should like it by nature. It is in your blood. You have your great-grandfather's highland red hair." They all nodded and smiled in appreciation.

My grandmother, who was the only non-sibling among the elders at the table, slowly pulled the bowl away. "There, there, we don't want you coming up with it if you can't eat it." With the hint of an Irish lilt that she had inherited from her family, she added, "Just eat the bacon and eggs Aunt Grace made just for you. Porridge can be an acquired taste." The others did not comment. They often told me that I looked like their dead father and that I walked like him and even phrased my conversation like him. He had been the first to arrive in Canada almost seventy years before. He had been a shepherd in the very north of Scotland, where the wall of Britain drops into the white lace tides of the frigid Arctic seas. He had walked all the way to Aberdeen to decide if he would leave the green rolling hills of Caithness for New Zealand, to work with the sheep, or for Canada. The matter was decided by the cost. He'd only had enough money to get to Canada. All the way across the Atlantic, tossed in the belly of an old sailing ship, he worried and wondered if there would be sheep in Ontario. He soon discovered that there were not enough sheep to make a decent living.

While he was labouring in an orchard he met a young woman and fell in love. She taught him to read and knew that someday he would make something of himself. As she lay exhausted from childbirth with their dead son in her arms, she asked him what day it was. It was the first of January. "I shall always be with you to guide you and yours on your journeys," she said as her voice weakened to a whisper and life faded from her, "from the first until the end…"

That breakfast when I gagged on the lumpy porridge was the last meal those siblings would enjoy together. I can imagine them now as children in their cramped house at the end of Carleton Street, all eight of them from their father's second marriage, some sleeping cross-wise in the double beds. Following the death of his first wife, their father had met a young school teacher who not only fell in love with him and married him, but who taught him arithmetic and the finer points of writing so he could become a policeman. His pursuits of criminals became legendary in Toronto. During the summer, the eight children—the five girls and the three sons—would go with their mother to a small cottage on Ward's Island. Their summer rituals were being reborn as the breakfast dishes disappeared and one by one the siblings slipped into their rooms to change into their bathing suits.

"We're all going to have our baths now," Hazel announced to me and waited to see the reaction on my face. Bea was too old. She said to go in without her, because the cold water bothered her arthritis. She promised to watch from the verandah where she sat enthroned in a groaning wicker chair with a commanding view of Lake Simcoe. One by one, the aunts emerged, dressed in bathing attire—not suits, but black dresses that frilled out at the waist and tied behind their necks with broad strings. Hazel's costume had short leggings. Grace pointed at the bloomers. "You really should get a new bathing suit, Hazel." Hazel turned to me. "I've had this suit for years, and it stands up better than all the new ones." We walked down to the shoreline. A plaid sunhat that did not match my plaid trunks was placed on my head, and a bulky orange life jacket was strapped on me because I did not yet know how to swim. My grandfather appeared through the screen door and his sisters shouted at him, "Bill, you'll have to roll up your long johns." His white Stanfield leggings were miles below his trunks. I thought he looked like a hockey player. At the water's edge, he bent and rolled them up, unable to hear what his sisters were saying because he had removed his hearing aid.

As the procession entered the water, the aunts' skirts ballooned out beneath them and bubbles of air rose out of their bodices. Grace carried me into the cold water and set me floating among them as they gathered in a circle. Flora, who had been quiet and worried about something most of the morning, produced a bar of Ivory soap and proceeded to scrub her arms and her neck before floating the soap to Grace, who in turn sent it off like a toy boat to Hazel. I had never been in a bath with other people, and when the soap came my way, I told them that I preferred to bathe alone. A great holler went up. "This is how we always did it at the island when we were children," said Flora.

"I'm going to teach you how to row later," my grandfather said, the white top of his outfit glowing in the morning sun through the gold-green ripples of the lake. The aunts fell silent.

My grandfather realized what he had said and a far away, grave look came over his face.

"It was a day like this, as I recall," said Hazel. Flora and Grace nodded. "It was this day," my grandfather said—he'd heard what they'd said through the curtain of his deafness because the words were surrounded by the silence of the moment, the stillness of the sisters in the lake. "It was this very day, July 1." And then I saw my grandfather start to sob. My grandmother swam up to him and touched his shoulder.

"You should know the story," Hazel said as she reached out and floated me closer to her. "Our eldest brother, Jim, was seventeen years old. He was training to be an electrician in Toronto and had come over to the island for the Dominion Day weekend. There was no phone over there. Late on the Friday night, he was doubled over in pain, and by morning he was gasping."

"We don't need all the details," said Flora.

"I just want the boy to know. Anyways, our father was in the city on his policeman's beat, and our mother was all alone with the gang of us in that little cottage. Your grandfather was our only hope because there weren't any doctors on the island. Your grandfather rowed across the bay in a little skiff we had, tied it up at Yonge Street, climbed a rope to the dock, and ran all the way up town to the old Wellesley Hospital for a doctor. He pleaded and pleaded for someone to come, but because it was a long weekend, they were short of doctors. Eventually, a young intern took pity on him and agreed to help. Your grandfather rowed the doctor back to the island. The doctor said Jim's appendix had to come out. They put Jim, who was now unconscious, and our mother and the doctor in the tiny skiff, and your grandfather rowed all the way back across the bay. When they got to the foot of Yonge, your grandfather's hands were a mass of bleeding blisters. He was told to wait at the rowboat. A few hours later, Mother appeared all by herself, her eyes reddened with tears for her lost first-born. Jim's appendix had burst, and it had been too late to save him even before they'd left the island."

"That was a first of July none of us will ever forget," added Flora. The telephone rang in the cottage. Bea was too bulky to get up easily to answer it, so my grandmother ran from the lake and got the receiver after many rings. She emerged onto the porch. "You'd better all come here. Please come here."

As Bea staggered in and the others clutched towels around their shoulders, my grandmother broke the news, "Isobel has passed away." Isobel was the one sister who was not present that day at the cottage. She was doing inventory at her husband's general store just north of Toronto when she suddenly dropped from a heart attack. A dark silence hung over the room. Quietly, the aunts retreated to their rooms. "You'd better pack up your things," my grandmother said. "We will all have to return to the city."

"Has anyone phoned Robert?" asked Bea. Robert was my grandfather's younger brother, who had decided to forego the reunion and spend time in Hamilton with his newest bride, his second wife. My grandmother told us that he had already been contacted by Isobel's sons.

As the group shuffled out the door on the way to their cars, letting the screen snap shut behind them, Flora turned and said, "It is the curse of the first come back among us." Hazel looked at her as if to silence her, but not before she added, "Our father died on the first of October, our mother on the first of March, and I know that this shall not be the last of the firsts."

In the days following the death of my aunt, I learned to listen to and understand grief. At family gatherings, where I scarcely knew who was who in the greater family, I tasted slices of slightly over-done banana bread. That sweet, burnt taste became the hallmark of many future gatherings after funerals. I drank my first cups of tea, watered to the point of sickliness, with milk and sugar. Death, to me, was overpoweringly sweet to taste and heavily scented with the perfume of peonies and lilies and widowed aunts.

As a child among the mourning adults, I watched as grief absorbed into their hearts and emerged as a pledge to keep life for the living. I listened as they tried to clutch tightly the laughter and stories that keep the spirits of dead family members alive. Yet beneath the laughter that emerged from the tears at the gatherings, a sense that something … someone … was missing presented itself like a shadow passing over the sun and darkening a room. And all the time, there were whispers about the curse of the first returning to the family.

They would turn to each other under hushed breath when they thought no one was listening and say things like, "Perhaps Father had remarried too soon after the death of his first bride." Perhaps there was an old wrong that needed to be righted. Perhaps the curse was something they had carried with them from the misty hills of Caithness, something hidden in the lost Gaelic tongue.

Two months later to the day, on the first of September, the telephone rang at my grandparent's house, where my father and mother and sister and I were gathered for Sunday dinner. Bea had passed away during her afternoon nap. And on the first of November, my mother woke me early in the morning to tell me that Flora had followed her elder sister. The first snow was falling as my grandfather stood at the window of his living room, saying nothing, his hands clasped in prayer, and his elbow leaning on his dark television set.

And on it went: Robert's eldest son departed on New Year's Day. Uncle Robert, shaken and bent like a windblown tree, asked why he should outlive his child. I got myself a calendar and stared at the empty white boxes as if they were questions waiting to be answered by the sound of a telephone ringing or an elder cousin appearing at the door in a suit and tie.

The first of every second month came with grim news until only my grandfather, grandmother, Robert, Grace, and Hazel remained of the large, smiling family I saw in the portrait that hung in the hallway of my grandparent's house. And, though so many were gone, I could still see them in my memory of the sunny gathering at Lake Simcoe. I prayed every night that everyone else would be spared. But the curse settled on Grace, as well as members of the next generation, until only Robert, Hazel, and my grandfather, with my grandmother by his side, stood alone against the darkness. For several months, almost eight, the dreaded cycle seemed to stop, and a collective sigh was uttered among the family. Perhaps the curse had run its course.

❧

Late the following summer, my grandfather fell ill, and sure enough, early on the morning of September the first, I awoke to the news that he had passed away. Robert stood over the coffin, weeping, and Hazel, who had by then almost completely lost her hold on reality, stared ahead and greeted me as if I was her father. "Can you make this stop, Father?" she asked with a pleading in her eyes that frightened me. I did not know what to say but instead hugged her and held her and whispered, "It will stop, it will stop."

On the way home from the cemetery, I saw through my grand-mother's black veil a look of stern determination. Her lips pursed. There were moments when her stoicism stood out and made her seem like a stone wall. When I was a child and my parents were angry at me, angry enough to want to spank me, I would take refuge behind my grandmother, who would protect me and plead my case. She was a rock of ages. I wanted her to protect me as much as I wanted to protect her, and I prayed quietly and secretly to God that she would do so, and that I would have the courage to alter the cycles of life that, like clockwork, were being imposed on those I loved. I was only six, and I was frightened. I reached out and took her hand across the seat of the limousine.

"I want you to live forever."

"No one lives forever, and you mustn't ask them to do so."

Later that evening, after I had climbed into bed, my grandmother, who'd decided to spend the next several days at my parents' house, came and sat on the edge of my bed. My grandmother sensed my fear. She must have seen it in my eyes as I sat quietly at the dinner table, unable to eat as my carrots grew colder and colder. Though I was only a child, she was aware that I knew about the curse, that

I'd overheard what the grown-ups said to each other funeral after funeral. I wanted desperately to hold on to the people I loved and the world I knew. I wanted those summer mornings at Lake Simcoe with the light shimmering off the gentle flow and the trees of Georgina Island guarding our moment proudly in the distance. Childhood is the one time in life when a person has the right to ask for such things: for stability and love and for constant familiarity. Eventually we have to make such things happen through the strength of our love for others and a refusal to be bullied by the realities of life.

My grandmother began to say a little prayer she often said over me when I stayed at her home. The prayer was a wish that I would grow in wisdom and in stature, and that God would watch over me all the days of my life and guide me in the face of darkness and despair. And before she added the final amen, she patted my cheek and said, "And for your sake I will not die on the first." Together we both said, "Amen."

My grandmother lived on for many years, and eventually followed my grandfather one September afternoon. Not long before she lost consciousness, she asked me what day it was, and I told her it was the fourth of September. She smiled and nodded, and I saw a look of protective love in her eyes as she whispered and squeezed my hand, "Good then, I will break the curse of the first forever." And she was the first who did not follow the others, the first to look the angel of death in the eye and say, "Not now, not today, I will in my own time, but it will be my own time." I repeat those words not only on the first day of every month, but each day when I rise, determined in the swim of life to stay afloat as best I can for those I love more than life.

The Watch

We simply disappear, maybe not in a puff of smoke or as a shadow down some dark alley, but in a trail of remnants that can either be reassembled and read, for what they are worth, or simply ignored and left to the ravages of time. And Mrs. Fermanagh knew that. When the adjutant officer came to her house one October afternoon in 1919, he handed her the watch. She opened the small razor box in which the timepiece had made its way home. She held it for a few moments in the hollow of her warm hand and handed it back to the regiment's man. It is now framed, rather awkwardly and inelegantly, in an oak casket in the local military museum. Within a few years she had forgotten it was there.

Time stands still. The barn is musty and stacked with antiques. A July wind tries to wheedle its way between the slats and the gaps in the crumbling foundation. Among the dampish upholstery and trashy relics of lives, he is staring out from his domed oval frame. He is another of the lost ones, an unknown soldier who speaks for those who cannot be found. His eyes beckon. He wants to please someone.

The photographer has hand-tinted the image so that the sitter's blue eyes and the gold maple leaf on his officer's forage cap pop from the greyish-blue background and his drab green tunic.

He is buttoned down. The corners of his mouth want to smile. Is this someone anyone would want to know? Is anyone curious about his trimmed moustache and why he grew it? Does it make him look older?

Listen.

The mice are scuttling to and fro in an old dresser. There are keyholes for each drawer. The key is missing. Jiggle the fronts. One drawer refuses to open. All the nameless faces in the discarded portraits are standing watch.

He would be late getting Anne back to Dalston. No one had wanted the tobogganing to end. The sky was the colour of a sailor's jacket, though far less warm; gentle, almost perfectly spaced snow was falling among the pines. The windows of the hillside stone house cast a yellow glow onto the yard beside the horse shed, and the lawn glowed diamonds. His mother would worry. He looked at his watch.

The warmth of his arm had kept the watch alive all afternoon without a second being lost. At the crossroads of the Penetanguishene Road, he leaned over and found Anne's face buried deep within the enormous buffalo rug. In the moonlight he kissed her rosy cheek as the runners of the sleigh eased through the snow and sounded a hush to the fields. Nothing save the lovers' breaths and the muffled trot of the horse's hooves on the white road could be heard.

On the drive home from Port Elgin north to Owen Sound, the sun set toward the outline of the Bruce Peninsula and a rainbow formed over the harbour at Meaford. The soldier in the backseat, his delicate glass dome facing upwards, wrapped badly in last week's newspaper, could not see it.

Officer burials are solemn events. A Union Jack drapes the rough wooden box. Officers are accorded a coffin unlike the men from the lower ranks. Those men that can be spared for ceremonial detail stand around the open grave, their heads bowed. The padre's white chasuble drapes over the black and khaki of his uniform and flutters in the wind. The man of the cloth bows his head and permits the body to surrender its spirit unto God. The guards say Amen. They raise their rifles and release a volley into the churchyard's sky, then lay their weapons where their shovels had been and return the earth to the earth. Fluttering ash descends from the sky because blanks are wadded with paper. The floating skein burns to a grey snowflake and lands on a private's sleeve without the soldier noticing it is there.

There is no time in war. No time to live. No time to remember, though there is time to die. The Bible says as much in Ecclesiastes. He keeps his watch wound. It is important that he never be late for anything. It is impossible to be early in Flanders. The roads are choked with men going up the line or down, with horses floundering and suffering on the crushed and bloody road as they haul their guns or wagons.

As far as the eye can see, men and animals are going nowhere with incredible determination. The stench of cordite is heavy in the air.

In the grey haze of dishevelled senses, he pulls back the sleeve of his great coat and checks the time. The watch had been a graduation present from his mother. He had stood with the other Officers' Training Core men in their uniforms, draped in their black gowns and hoods outside Convocation Hall. His mother peered into the viewfinder of her box camera. Her world appeared upside-down. He stood with his chums, leaning against the truncated plinth that marked the spot Sir Sanford Fleming had declared the centre of time.

For a few brief moments before departing England for France, the group had stood astride the Greenwich Meridian. He knew as they made their way across the Channel to the French coast that they must have crossed it again; only this time, the minutes and the seconds were as useless to him as the regimental sabre his uncle had passed to him as a family symbol of loyalty and service to the Crown.

The military records indicate that the bombardment that took the life of Mrs. Fermanagh's son happened shortly before midnight, in preparation for a German raid of the Canadian line.

As usual, the young officer had wound his watch at noon that day. According to the notebook kept by the company's captain, everything was running according to schedule.

The hour hand of the watch in the regimental museum is distinctly pointing to four o'clock although the crystal is missing along with the minute hand. Like the famous Hiroshima watch from World War II, the Fermanagh watch should have ceased to keep time at the moment of explosive impact. The hour hand should point a little past eleven, and even accounting for the fact that the bombardment's precise time may have been delayed by several minutes, it should have registered no more than a few millimeters beyond the eleven on the watch's dial. The discrepancy between the time of death and the time registered on the watch could be attributed to several things.

First theory: someone, on removing the wristwatch from what was left of the young officer's arm, had tapped it. Or, perhaps the watch had rattled in the box on its journey from Flanders to London to his hometown, each knock coaxing another moment in time from its shattered body. As it made its way home, it shuffled with the photograph he carried in his right breast pocket of Anne, an artifact the museum keeps in a storage box away from the public because it is smeared in the brownish veneer of old blood. Or maybe someone with few scruples in a transit office opened the box to see if the timepiece was still working, tapped it, and nudged a few more precious hours into the measure of a life that had already reached its conclusion.

Second theory: the wristwatch, shattered as it was with damage to the mainspring and cogs, kept up its persistent pulse even after it had ceased to function as a reliable instrument, and simply wound down four hours after its partial destruction. As time flowed, the watch bled seconds until it simply ran down to silence. That would account for the four hours of additional time after its partial destruction, though if still working, the watch should have wound down at noon. There is a third theory that needs to be addressed in the story of the watch.

Mrs. Fermanagh had refused to answer the door since the day the telegram arrived regretting to inform her of the death in battle of her only son, Lieutenant Charles Fermanagh, Grey and Simcoe

Foresters 177th Reg't (transferred)/10th Brigade, Princess Patricia's Light Infantry. She had no idea how long she lay in a heap on the floor of the vestibule after the telegram boy's departure. A winter chill blew in off Kempenfelt Bay and crept under the door.

On the October day in 1919 when the regimental representative came to present her with her son's relic, the sky was bright and clear, though a russet sunset was beginning to take shape in the west. The leaves were brilliant in their orange and yellow and red transformation.

She met the officer in the front parlour. She entered the room, and the soldier rose and snapped to attention. This frightened Mrs. Fermanagh. The family mansion on Sunnidale Road now felt emptier than ever, as if an echo longed to answer footsteps, and the floorboards had been told to hush. She held the watch for a few moments, staring into its broken face as if it was the visage of Christ lowered from the cross. Her eyes teared up but she said nothing. She wanted to feel the heartbeat, that tiny pulse of life that her gift of love and remembrance had once possessed. In the warmth of her palm, the hour hand may have moved, startled to life by unexpected contact with a sudden, familiar touch.

But the mud of Flanders refused to relinquish its grip on the mechanism. It clutched a million lives, and against its tenacious hold a small wristwatch stood no chance. The brown grains of a battlefield fall on the white conservation cloth when the watch is taken from its oak frame for examination at the museum. The winder is jammed. As it is, the hour hand could not have moved past one or two o'clock. Something inside the watch was frozen at the fourth hour of a day that never completely began.

Having stopped there, the hour hand stands pointing forever to the number four, on guard and almost saluting to that precise, inexplicable moment.

After taking Anne all the way home to Dalston in the cutter, having promised his mother he would not let the horse and the girl freeze to death in a ditch along some dark and haunted concession, Charles Fermanagh arrived home. The moonless dark of night was still heavy in the pines that lined the road and chilling to the point he could no longer feel his thighs and hands. His mother heard the key turn in the door and stood at the top of the staircase, peering down into the hall.

"You're home safe?"

"Yes. I had a wonderful time."

"I've been worried. I've been all night on the watch, waiting for you. I thought you were dead in a ditch or frozen solid in an empty field somewhere."

"I would have been in sooner, but I wanted to stow the cutter and harness in the shed and give Maddie a thorough fodder and brushing down to ease the ice off her."

"What did Anne's parents say? They should have let you stay the night rather than risk the roads all the way back."

"It wasn't that far. Just to Dalston. I think they were happy I got her home safely. They were glad her fiancé had got her home in one piece as promised, although a bit after the fact. Can't help winter travel."

"Fiancé? Isn't that a bit of a rush? Does she know what she's getting into? You're leaving in a few weeks. She hardly knows you, and we have not yet met her parents."

"I don't really care," he said as he stepped out of his fur-topped galoshes and hung his coat and scarf on the hall tree. "I don't really care. Life is too short. It's never long enough."

"I hope you know what you are doing."

"Well, even if I don't, time will tell."

"Go to bed now," she admonished. She turned and ascended the stairs, and he, almost her shadow, followed.

The fourth runner on the staircase to the warmer climes of his familiar room creaked beneath his foot. And the clock in the parlour chimed four times into the darkness as if someone, someday, would be listening.

Boiling Point

Gwen stared out the window at the blizzard and waited for the courier to come with Maggie's precious insulin pills. She thought about the trail dogs that once ran to deliver medicine to remote communities such as hers and was reminded of the name of the first encyclopaedist. Iditarod. Diderot.

Moving here from the city had been Dave's idea. The telephone company needed linemen, and they offered to double his pay.

Thin wires of conversation stretched along the old logging roads and hydro clear cuts. She had been playing tin-can telephone with Mags on a morning like this when she received word that Dave had slipped and fallen from a repeater station early the night before. He had lain in the snow through long lonely hours, his cellphone useless because he had shut down the tower to repair it. The weather gradually crept inside him, leaving a starry patch among the snow-laden pines and silence on his phone.

One very cold day when Gwen was eight, her mother put a pot on the stove to boil. She called the girls into the kitchen as steam clouds rose. "Open the back door!" she exclaimed. "I'm going to show you a miracle!" With the door wide open, Gwen had felt the deep chill wrap its arms around her. Her mother took the pot and flung the contents into the air. In an instant, the scalding liquid became snow.

Mags walked into the kitchen in her sleepers. Her face was grey, and her forehead was covered in beads of cold sweat. The mother and daughter exchanged glances that betrayed the fact that both knew, almost instinctively, that the situation was growing more dire by the minute.

A pot of hot water that Gwen had put on for tea was mumbling on the stove.

"Let me show you something," Gwen said, trying to cheer her child. She grabbed the pot from the burner and set it momentarily on the countertop beside the kitchen door. With a push, she was able to force the door over the newly stacked snow that tried to bar her inside the house. Mags approached cautiously as Gwen picked up the pot of steaming water.

"Watch," she said to the child. "Mommy is going to make magic." The air, as she breathed in, hardened inside her nose to the point that she could almost feel her head crack. She flung the water into the air above the small porch, and instantly it became a reeling cloud of steam.

Mags gasped and Gwen dropped the pot of water as Dave's pale shadow appeared in the sudden whir of snowflakes, his hands empty and reaching out to them.

A Chronicle of Magpies

One for Sorrow

The last light was still falling on the sofa in the parlour as he pleaded his case: "I have been told to leave everything in the city and go somewhere to grow potatoes." In his words Julia heard the end of a story rather than the beginning of a new one. She felt her feathers ruffled. He repeated, "I have to go somewhere and grow potatoes or my ulcer will kill me."

Julia thought he was exaggerating. Many things had not killed Michael Gorman. He'd fought in the Great War and survived. The Great Fire that had taken his father's printing business, along with most of downtown, had not broken him. And when fire, omnipresent fire, destroyed their first home and everything they owned, they'd moved into her sister's house and carried on. None of these struggles had brought with them the same sense of finality. Julia pulled her black cardigan tighter around her white blouse. This was a silence that stared into the future. This was an incautious step on thin ice.

Julia gazed into her hands as they lay folded in her lap, palms upward as if they were bowls of milk in which she might see the future. "We're starving now," she replied, her voice not rising above a flat whisper.

"But think of it this way, Julia … we can grow our own food."

"Potatoes? Do you think we're Irish?"

She looked at him and wanted to laugh him into the floor, but her face remained steely. She would have to leave her job, the only income the family had. She would have to say goodbye, yet again, to the friends and family she had in the city. She didn't mind living at her sister's. In fact, as the older of the two siblings, she had made the place a domain of her own, ordering her mother and niece around in the kitchen and directing dinner in the same way she managed the employees at the restaurant downtown. In her mind, all she could see ahead were the days as flat and furrowed as potato fields. She envisioned the long winters when snow would fill in the corduroy plough lines and stub stalks of a rough harvest and imagined the taste of boiled spuds that echoed the metallic flavour of the pot they were cooked in. Instead of just two mouths to feed, there would be three by the time they got to his potato field. She could imagine the wind's longing to rest its weariness in whatever remote place Michael would take them. It was the wind that she feared most. She could imagine it crossing the fields with its merciless cavalry of snow devils in the dead of winter. And there would be footprints in the earth of those who had struggled there and lost the battle before them, the ghosts of the house despairing at what they had lost and what she and Michael would lose.

A week later, Michael came home—from where she could not guess—and she kissed him so she could smell his breath and see if he had been visiting a bootlegger. He had not. His skin smelled of the singe, coal, and automobile exhaust that said he had been downtown.

"We have a place to live," he beamed as he took her in his arms. "A place to live!"

Where was it, she questioned, and who had lived there and why did they fail and is this what we really need … and why did you buy something without going to look at it first, you fool, you fool. Michael sat her down, held her hands with a frantic enthusiasm that scared her, and gave her the details.

The land had been a family farm. It had belonged to a woman whose husband had been killed in France. Since the war, a cousin of hers had worked the acreage with the hope that when her son was old enough, he could decide whether he wanted it. But the woman needed the money and needed it now. With what little Julia and Michael had saved, money from the sale of their few belongings, and a small assistance from his granduncle, Michael purchased the potato field deep in the northern bush. *But, oh my, oh my,* she shook her head and thought to herself, *he really took the doctor at his word.*

Michael had never been an easy man to live with. He would turn at night and mutter in his sleep. His sweats just before dawn unnerved her—he soaked the bed from head to foot. Following the fire that took their first home, he had shaken for days. They'd lost everything, including his nerve. She often thought about that night, the flames leaping from the second floor of their new house, their things—things that they had gathered as symbols of their future life together—vanishing in the tongues of red and orange and the billows of black smoke before their lives together had really begun. They had married only six weeks after his return from the war. Their families, hard on the heels of their wedding, had done what they could for them.

One of the few things that survived the fire was a family heirloom, a painting of the Humber River where she and Michael had gone canoeing on a lazy summer afternoon in the days following his return. On the banks of the Humber stood the ruins of the old mill, a sad and picturesque shell of the promises that had once been part of an idyllic world. When she'd visited her cousin's house during the years the men were away, she would sit and stare at the painting and almost believe that the ripples of the flow were running toward her, alive with the beauty of a time that was now forever lost. She imagined she would go there with Michael when the war was over, his paddle lifting tiny silver drops from the river, the motion of the water beneath her edging up through her spine, the sun and the intervals of breeze stroking her forehead. In her imagination, she looked up from the cushions in the cradle of that canoe and saw Michael's silhouette outlined before her, his young shoulders swaying as he put the water behind him, and she thought to herself, *I am happy*. Even though they'd only shared a few moments together years before, Julia decided that Michael would be her husband if he asked her. During the years of waiting that seemed to stretch out like the ocean, there had been only censored, cryptic postcards that said nothing and contained no personal messages and the daily papers with their lists of dead and wounded filling columns across a no-man's land of ink and paper.

What had happened to him in those years? When he returned from the war, there had been a strange scent to his skin as they danced together at a fashionable party in a Rosedale mansion. She pressed close to him, having dreamt throughout the years he had been away that he would be close to her. As she turned her nose toward his shirt collar, she caught the faint hint of singe and looked up and saw not warmth in his eyes, but a distance that troubled her. Their wedding had been as she had wanted it. Her father's Rosedale garden was in full bloom. She had come to the realization that nothing would be the same after the war, but the sight of the roses opening on the morning of her wedding—each one sparkled with dewdrops that had gathered in the early hours of the dawn—and the brilliant sunlight emerging through the maples and scattering a fortune of golden coins on the shining grass gave her such hope.

Michael had said nothing as the flames licked through the roof of their home. Neighbours ran back and forth, shouting instructions to the firemen. He just stood there. Several times she saw him look down and paw the ground with the toe of his shoe, and silently she had clutched at his arm to comfort him. Then came the fire in Rawlinson's Storage downtown, and the last shreds of their lives, the foundations of what seemed like starting over, also went up in flames.

Her mother, who was as indefatigable as spring, had taken the trolley to the warehouse where the firemen were sifting through the ashes. She'd crossed the barrier against the protests of police and firemen and insurance adjusters and reporters: a woman in the black dress of a widow, picking up the hem of her skirt and wading into the sea of ashes. "My daughter's life is in there," she yelled back at the admonishments for her safety. The onlookers feared she would be burned alive by a loose spark or a curling ember that steadfastly refused to surrender its destructive spirit. Within ten minutes, however, Julia's mother emerged clutching an armload of things. "I knew just where you had left the trunk," she told Julia with resolute pride that evening as she sat at her kitchen table and displayed the retrieved fragments of her daughter's life: the Irish linen tablecloth and the picture of the Humber her cousin had given her as a wedding gift.

The cloth, like a sacred relic, had emerged from the fire almost unscathed except for a small scar of crisping on one corner. "You can probably wash that out," noted the old woman as she held the frail, beige knots between her fingers. The two women sat and gazed at the painting of the Humber. It too seemed a miracle. The current still flowed forward, refusing even in the extreme heat to stem its cooling tide. The birds that had been in flight over the river, a painter's afterthoughts, had darkened. "They don't look like gulls anymore," Julia said with a sigh.

"Magpies," her mother responded quickly. "Those are magpies. There are two of them there. Two means there will be joy. Think of them as thieving phoenixes. They stole their lives from the flames and are coming now to greet you. Hang it with pride in your new home. It will bless you."

Upon arrival at the farmhouse, Michael pulled off the brown paper wrapper that enshrouded the frame and hung the river scene on a nail he found protruding from the blank wall of what had been the parlour. He thought it might cheer Julia. It would be, as all pictures should be in a home, a window onto another world. It did not cheer Julia in the least.

What distracted her during those first days when it rained and rained was the view from the real windows. After three days that seemed more like forty to her, the rain ceased and Michael could discover, at last, what there was of his new kingdom.

When Julia stood at the window, all she could hear was silence, deafening, deadening—everything seemed to have come to a stand-still with a dull thud. A scrivener pine stood and watched her from the clearing that was supposed to be their backyard. She allowed herself the fantasy that the yard would need lilacs. Lilacs could be stolen from the wilderness. But the pine seemed to moralize on the point. The pen-like tree bent forward as if it wanted to tell her something and listened for her reply. She did not speak its language. She was used to the sounds of the city: the horses clomping on the streets, the backfire of rattling taxis, and the heaving sighs of trucks huffing down the avenue. She was used to knowing the life of things as they spoke to her, and here, where everything was green, life lay hidden in things and refused to remove its mask. Her heart sank.

She waited and waited at the window until suddenly a promising sign appeared. It was Michael. He was stomping around in the mud and pacing off the field with his survey in hand. *That fool will be the death of me*, she thought, and if she died way out here, who would notice? All she wanted to do was to outlast it. Yet, here, there was something strangely enduring in the rocks and trees, the silences, the green, the endless, awkward green that filled every narrow patch and crack it could find. Michael, on the other hand, was fascinated by it all. For the first time since the war, he came to life. "This is a steal," he exclaimed. "This place is a steal." His survey map became the key to his new kingdom, and he poured over it during those first days of rain when they clung to their nest, as empty as it was, furnished only with anticipations, a lace tablecloth, a bed, a few chairs, and the painting of the Humber. When he left Julia standing in the echoing, wooden-walled rooms of the farmhouse, he felt a sense of pity toward her, but also a tremendous urgency to know what was his.

He returned to the back stoop that was little bigger than a gallows and pointed out the weed patch he would have to clear, where the crops of potatoes would again rise from the brown and melancholy earth. He would take possession of it all, he said with pride and determination. It was his, or rather, theirs. She simply looked at him, pursed her lips, and shook her head.

The dense thicket and the outstretched arms of the cedars and pines, the cobwebbed branches of scrub oak and undernourished birches could not hold him back. On the far right-hand side of his survey was an irregular line underscored with the words *shore waste* scrawled in draftsman's hand. And when he stumbled over a protruding rock and fell to the ground, the survey slipped from his hands and blew back in his face as he tried to stand up. He stood, pulled the mask of the map down to his chest, and there before him was what he had been searching for all his life. The slate-grey sky opened above the calm, dark lake, blue out far and delicately tea-coloured in close where the rocks vanished like ghosts into the depths. Gnats danced in the still air, and from a ring of ripples he saw the head of a loon rise to breathe and then disappear beneath the surface. Suddenly, the sun broke through the clouds and scattered diamonds across the surface of the water. The lake was untouched by time or man, and the shoreline of the bay he now owned stretched around the waters like great welcoming arms while an honour-guard of virgin-growth pines stood on their sentry duty, protecting his new secret. He had found paradise.

The problem with paradise, Julia pointed out to him that evening as they sat down to a meal of boiled things, was that paradise was not real and that every Eden always fell no matter how hard one tried to hold on to it. He told her she was a pessimist. He told her he had paced the shoreline out and there was more land by that water than in any field of potatoes. She told him not to gesticulate with his knife and fork and that his dinner was getting cold.

"But I've seen it, I've seen it," he replied.

He knew she was right in her own way, and she became even more right as the snow fell on the fields, closing off the road to the nearest town, stranding them in their tiny ark of a farmhouse. The wind howled, especially on the night Julia gave birth to their first child. As she heard the wind cry in sympathy, she thought, *Yes, you and I are kindred in this horror.* It too was lonely and stranded in this remote place.

Michael had gone for the doctor, and out her window she could see a bent pine, hunched over in the gusts, and momentarily, between attacks of infinite, ungodly hurt, she imagined that her husband had turned into one of those pines, his face pointing permanently to the east where the lake lay frozen.

By the time Michael returned with the doctor it was too late to save his newborn son, so they just did what they could for Julia.

A heavy rain was falling on the road from Dainville to Arras in the dark hours just before day awoke on that August morning in 1918. In the darkness, the Canadian Corps slowly shuffled their way forward so that they would be parallel with the bulge in the line that protruded to the west. The column came to a halt where two lorries had slid and overturned in the mud. The guns had been eerily quiet since dinner the previous evening, and the sound of hundreds of feet sucking at the road that turned into a pudding beneath the weight of the advancing army reminded Michael Gorman of frogs he had heard in the dawn while fishing along the Grand.

The men were under pain of punishment not to speak in the lines for fear that the enemy would hear them, though the enemy was far off to their right, two, three miles away in the darkness. Michael turned to the man beside him and saw the profile of his best mate, also named Michael, as the rain flowed along the eaves of his friend's helmet and streamed down onto his tunic. His friend looked pale, and steam seemed to be rising from his shoulders. During the halt, the sergeant made his way back among the brigade and spoke in a low voice.

"Gorman?"

"Sir!"

"Is Philips still with us?"

"Yes, sir!"

"He looks pale. Do you feel pale, Philips?"

"No, sir!"

"Bloody hell, you are." He put his hand to Philips' forehead. "You're running a fever."

"Sir!"

"I said, you're running a goddamned, bloody fever!"

"Sir!"

"You're going to visit the rear when we arrive at our stationing point."

"Sir!"

"Carry on!"

The two Michaels turned and looked at each other.

"Are you—"

Suddenly, out of nowhere, a whirring whistle screamed down on them and came apart in all directions. Men flung themselves into a huddled crouch on the road-bed instinctively, as if together they would all be protected. A whistle blew. The sergeant who had just been beside them waved his arm madly toward a large blur of trees that were slowly articulating themselves out of the darkness toward their right. The two Michaels rose from their knees and hurled themselves down the bank of the road and through the ditch and the low field beyond which a copse of dark welcomers waited to protect them. Gorman turned and looked back at where the column had been. The sergeant was standing dumbfounded on the road over a man who was bent double and clutching his stomach. And with that, both figures toppled over, motionless.

Philips was breathless as he reached and wrapped his arms around a tree as if it were receiving him with love. Gorman caught up and pulled him to the ground. For a few moments, the two lay there and stared into each other's blank gazes as the green and orange flashes of the bombardment lit their faces, engulfing them in the lightning and thunderclaps of the shell bursts. Gorman reached up and wiped something from his mouth. It was metallic and raw tasting, and in the flashes he and Philips saw that it was red and orange with bits of dirt and gravel in it. Gorman spat it into his muddy palm and began to choke. He rolled to his side and vomited into the frail shreds of grass at the base of the tree and then rolled back into Philips' arms. The ground continued to shake violently and Philips held on for dear life. The road where they had been was alive with flames and smoke and screaming horses and crying men.

As quickly as the melee had started, it stopped. Philips shook with a chill, Gorman sobbed on his shoulder, and the two remained in their embrace as a lieutenant crawled up to them on the ground. He was completely covered in mud, monochromatic the length of his body except for the gold tie pin that still held his four-in-hand in place. It glinted in the moonlight that now filtered through the wood.

"On my signal," whispered the officer as if there was something secretive about his plan that he did not want the others or the enemy to overhear, "we will stand up and advance in a slow march through the woods in an easterly direction. We'll reassemble when we reach the next major break in the trees, and I'll take roll there and reorganize us." With that, he crawled away, still desperately holding on to the earth as if it might leave him.

The two men on their stomachs listened; an hour passed. The birds were beginning to chirp again in their first chorus of the day, retaking their territory. Gorman looked around and could see, in the dense fog, the first shards of light into which the corps would walk. All around him, shadows slowly stood into the broken lances of daybreak that now outlined them all, and from where he lay it seemed as if the dead had awakened from their tombs and, in a great resurrection, faced east to Jerusalem and slowly and solemnly began to walk toward it, bayonets fixed.

Together the Michaels had each worn out three pairs of boots, had felt the hobnails scrape on the stones of Amiens as they washed back and forth from the hard won ground of the Somme and Vimy and Passchendaele to the new frontline that separated the junction city of Arras from the next nerve centre of Cambrai, and beyond that Douai and the German frontier. In the no-man's land where Picardie met Flanders, where the yellow-brown soil reddened with the blood of both armies, they had fought for three years and, remarkably, had survived. The German lines had broken. The soldiers that faced them were soft, pale boys whose faces, in the repose of death, seemed angelic and filled Michael with a grief he had not felt before.

Gorman turned and looked behind him. A flock of magpies had descended upon a small meadow where the grasses remained low among the late summer blossoms. There were so many birds— five, six, seven—that he had no time to count as he turned to face his officer and bend his ear toward the man's hushed words in the new day.

"Roberston." Silence. "Robertson. No? Rumsey."

"Sir!"

"Rushton. Sir."

"Sinclair."

"Sir."

At the end of the call, Gorman and Philips pressed forward. "Gorman and Philips, sir!"

"Gorman and Philips. You were late for roll."

"Philips is not well," Gorman announced. Philips looked at him with a sense of betrayal in his eyes.

"Philips?"

"A little slow, sir! None the worse for wear."

"Good. You two know the drill. We lost five sergeants back there. Bloody mess. I've never been in a spot where I've lost five sergeants, and we're not even into our ready positions. So, you two corporals are hereby promoted to lead squads. Gorman, you take six, Philips, you take seven. Understood? That's all." Philips and Gorman looked at each other and nodded in silence. Two days later, a whistle sounded and Michael Gorman and Michael Philips went forward, leading their men into the Battle of Arras. That was the day the Canadian Corps sent the German army into flight. It was the beginning of the end of the Great War.

❧

The view from the office window looked directly into the window of another office on Bay Street. Michael thought about how wealth was always looking in on itself like someone staring at their own face in a mirror. That was the way one kept the worth in things—by staring into them until they became one's own reflection. To become wealthy, however, was a different matter. To become wealthy, one had to look beyond things, like looking into the depths of the lake or a deep river. He always sensed when he looked into the depths there was something there that he ought to see, something to look back at him. He stood up from the leather couch as the frosted glass door of the private office in front of him opened.

"Mr. Gorman, do come in," the man in the three-piece suit motioned with his hand, pointing the way to a leather chair that sat in front of a large mahogany desk. The man sat down behind the desk, closed the cover on one file, and opened another. "I've looked through your proposal, and I can see some possibilities. You say you built this lodge with your own hands and that the fishing there is good?"

"Yes, right after we settled in, I set about clearing some of the space beside the lake, and with the trees that I felled, I thought, 'these are too good to waste.' It took some work, as you can see from the photographs, but we now have seven rooms, all with lakefront views, and a very large dock. I am next going to build a central lodge. My wife, who had a very good job as a restaurant manager here in the city, has been doing a fine job catering to the diets of some of our first customers."

"Well, looking at your past business record, you have a history of unlucky results with your enterprises. I suppose one cannot blame you for the fires and the bad luck that seems to have followed you. But one has to wonder if certain people simply don't have the touch sometimes."

"The touch?"

"Well, in business, I prefer to call it the foresight that allows one to see around corners, to see what is coming or could come."

"Mr. Pierce, there is no doubt that I have been touched by fire more than most men. I would like to believe that is behind me. The other point in my favour, of course, is that I am building a business on water now."

Pierce was silent for a moment as the playfulness of Michael's statement sank in. With a smile he looked up from the papers. "I realize that Mr. Gorman." Pierce sat back in his large swivel chair. He looked directly at Michael, sizing him up. "I have to say that our board liked your vision. That piece of potato land you're sitting on could become something intriguing. Lord knows that the old vacation spots of my time—Mimico, Long Branch—they've all been overrun by the city. They are too close and they've lost their lustre. Even Simcoe and Couchiching are getting, how shall we say, overstocked?" Michael nodded and Pierce continued.

"Money, as you know, is hard to come by these days. People are cautious. However, there are great plans for the north. The new ONR is a stroke of brilliance. The north is opening. Can you imagine that one day there will be communities stretching all the way from Toronto to Moose Factory?"

For a moment, Michael sensed that Pierce was off on a tangent of enthusiasm. Pierce cleared his throat.

"In any case, Mr. Gorman, our investors believe that the first phase of expansion will be into your area, and that your project is a safe proposition." He stood up, extended his hand, and looking Gorman in the eye, said, "We're pleased to be doing business with you."

As Michael walked up Bay Street, the hands of the city hall clock met as if they were praying at the stroke of noon, and the tower spoke. He stared at the face of the clock as it loomed over the financial avenue and thought, *Yes, thank God, things are looking up.* He dreamt that his paradise could become a haven for the city's rich. There had been so many comrades in the mud and filth just a few years before who had, in quiet moments between engagements, lain down beside him beneath a tree or in a hayloft and shared their dreams of what the perfect world might look like on the other side of the war. And now, for him, it would be possible. He could not have stomached any other result.

Michael walked east on Queen, strolling along the crowded streets until, on a densely packed avenue of ramshackle houses, he stood in front of a small house with a Gothic dormer cresting the front. The roof had become hunched and slung in on itself as if it were someone's collapsed dream. The front walls leaned outward and the neighbourhood smelled of cabbage. As he stood staring at the house, a boy with auburn hair appeared at the window, parting the greying lace curtains, pressing his fingers to the glass. Michael nodded to the boy as the drapes fell back across the window and the boy disappeared.

Michael stood at the edge of the house's front walk, but hesitated and changed his mind. This time he would not go into the house that seemed to wait for him like a stranger on a street corner. This was no time for sadness. He had so much to tell Julia. He turned on his heel at that instant and vanished along the street—his destination, the CP telegraph office on Richmond.

Julia STOP *Paradise* STOP

Michael returned the receiver to its cradle as Julia stuck her head into the office off the foyer of the new main lodge. "Is something wrong?" she asked. He shook his head, and Julia disappeared down the polished corridor, past the wicker settees and the plant stands. He had asked the woman on the telephone not to call him again and after a long silence the phone had gone dead. It would be better for all, he concluded, if she stayed in the city.

He remembered the beauty of her laughter, the good times he'd had with her and his best friend, Michael Philips, in the summer of 1914, before the world turned upside-down. The two Mikes had met Maggie at a church social. She had come along with a girl she knew from her work. But over the course of that hot July afternoon, when everyone knew that life would change, but that the boys would be home by Christmas, she'd forgotten her friend and latched herself to Philips and his best friend.

In the weeks leading up to the boys' enlistment, Maggie and the Michaels were inseparable. As the autumn leaves started to fall and word came from overseas that the Germans had reached the Marne, the world seemed to insist that the two Michaels be drawn into the twilight of enthusiasm and rage that day by day became a darkness. On a winter evening at the home of her uncle, Maggie walked down the staircase as the two Michaels stood before the parlour window and the minister. It was then that she took Michael Philips to be her husband. Three days later she waved goodbye to the boys as the train pulled out of Union Station and the snow fell thicker and thicker through the air until it swallowed the last departing car.

Months passed and the occasional letter would make its way back to the city. Maggie learned that the boys of the second contingent had been in England, in a training camp on Salisbury Plain, and that when Gorman had become ill with a stomach malady, Philips had checked on him every day in the infirmary to cheer his recovery. The Michaels shared a letter which Maggie had written to say that she was pregnant, and they huddled together in a driving spring rain as the trench in Flanders enveloped them in a thick yellow-grey ooze. Flanders, the Somme, Passchendaele, Vimy—the lines washed back and forth across the generals' maps. The faces in the ranks changed and changed until only two men were still familiar to each other. Only the two Michaels remained.

The morning of August the twenty-sixth, 1918, as the first green shred of dawn announced another foggy summer day, the air was both wet and hot and reminded Gorman of the breath of a dog. The enemy would not see them coming. A young officer looked down the line to his left and then to his right to make sure all the men were in place as the rows pressed their bodies against the ground of their position. He glanced at his watch, 4:19 a.m., then called along the line, "For all we love and for Canada!"—his cheeks exploded into balloons as he poured his soul into his three tone whistle and the bombardment from the rear buzzed overhead. From behind came a tremendous rumbling of the ground, followed by the ear-shattering timpani that cried around them like a siege of taunted herons. As they had drilled, they waited to rush screaming from their hiding place in the woods. Michael Gorman shouted at a shaking private to be still, and with that an enormous steel beast passed between them with the blasted passion of a banshee, its twin Vickers blazing a trail ahead as the squad clambered up over the low, makeshift parados and followed closely behind the hump-backed leviathan.

"Hunch low, squad six, stay low!" he shouted though he knew only the men closest could hear him over the motor of the land battleship. "Fall in behind the tank!"

Gorman looked to his left and saw the men of the seventh squad labouring forward, some hunched, some dropping to the ground. They had no tank to shield them. Where was their goddamned tank? Suddenly, squad seven vanished into a cloud of smoke that blew back upon the troops of the advancing bombardment.

As they approached the German line, Gorman peered around the side of the huge machine and saw no motion, no flashes of fire from the trench ahead, so he waved his arm in the air and wheeled his squad to the left where a Spandau's burst of flame licked out into no man's land. His men understood their purpose, and by the time he reached the lip of the trench, his men were firing into the pit. Gorman turned his head away as the last tap sounded from the captured gun.

Leaping into the trench, which was little more than a tangle of absurd objects and puzzle pieces that his mind strained to fit together, he stepped on something. It was the face of a young boy that lay buried in the mud. He did not want to see it. It seemed innocent and asleep, a mirror of something of himself that he could no longer stomach to look at, so he pressed the toe of his boot against it, hard, and almost made the soft cheek smile as it disappeared into the murk. That was the end, he thought.

A tumble of rafters and beams lay ahead of him, and he parted it. On and on they pressed that day, covering eight miles—the longest single Canadian advance of the war. He reached a field and bent over to catch his breath. It was hot and the sun had burned off the fog so that the day was brilliant. Beyond, he saw men in grey uniforms running from the scene, and an open planting of reddish-golden wheat, almost ripe, before them. It reminded him for a moment of Maggie's hair as she combed out the long strands during a picnic by the Humber.

❧

Several weeks after the heated telephone call, Julia appeared at Michael's office door. She was holding a letter in her hands.

"Michael, can you explain this?" She passed him the letter and he examined it. It was a letter from Maggie Philips.

He cleared his throat. "Yes, you know about Michael Philips. He was in my outfit in France. This is from his widow. I bought the property from her."

"She says she didn't know the property would be valuable."

"Nor could she," he answered quickly. "This was nothing. She couldn't even grow potatoes. It has been our hard work that made this resort what it is now. If she had stayed here," he stopped for a moment, passing his eyes over the rest of the letter and turning it in his hands, "she would have starved." He put the letter face down on his desk. "It is that simple. She bought the house in the city with the money from the farm. She needed a place to raise her son. At the time I thought we were getting the worse of the deal. We came here on doctor's orders. I don't see that she has cause to complain now."

49

Julia shrugged. "No, I suppose not," she said. "Is there anything we can do for her?"

"Well, I haven't wanted to tell you this, but I made a promise to Michael Philips during some rough going in France that I would look after his wife and child, and I have."

Julia wheeled around and looked at him with an incredulous look on her face. "You've helped them—how?" she said, her voice rising with anger.

"I helped her with her son. I've sent small amounts of money when I've been able to, and never when things were tight here."

"How much? Oh … I don't want to know. You can be generous at your expense, but not at ours, is that agreed? I have cooked for all these visitors. I have sawed lumber and raised beams when I've been pregnant. I had three miscarriages and lost a baby because we are in the middle of nowhere. My sister says I should have left you years ago. I feel as if the best years of my life have been stolen from me because of your dreams and your needs. And you haven't got the guts to tell me about this woman? You bastard! Is that who you visit when you go off to the city? I am not going to be shortchanged because you feel sorry for someone I've never met."

"Well, I am sorry," said Michael, a sad look on his face. "A soldier's promise is a soldier's promise. All these things keep eating away inside me. The war has been over a long time, and I suspect she's almost on her feet now. She had a tough time of it these past years, but things are going to improve."

"I should have been so lucky as to march beside you. Are you telling me the whole story about her?"

Michael smiled. "Secrets, thousands and thousands of secrets. A veritable king's ransom's worth of secrets. I keep them on the bottom of the lake. Treasure is best when it's buried."

"I don't know what you mean, and by the way, I am pregnant again," said Julia as she turned back toward the foyer to greet an arriving visitor from the city.

"Mr. Carruthers. How charming to see you again."

❦

Young Irene sat and watched as her parents tugged at the ends of a lumber saw, back and forth, in the late spring heat, until finally Michael looked at his wife, thin, exhausted, and seemingly years older than her actual age, and decided to dip into the loan that Pierce and Carruthers and their business partners had offered him. Within a few months, with the work of men from the town who were finding it a struggle to make ends meet in the northern economy, the new hotel addition to the lodge, with its fieldstone floors and cobblestone fireplace, had risen into the daylight of the cutting. The first pines and cedars that Michael had parted, with his map in hand, were clear cut, and the view beyond them was of the blue lake named for a man called Harper who had disappeared into the mists of time without so much as a footnote in the history of the area, other than his name on the map.

"They should name the lake after me," Michael had declared one night over dinner as he spooned his soup.

"How about me too?" asked Julia. A silence descended on the room as they sat and finished their dinner. A new map was drawn up by the local council when they incorporated the bush and the lake into the new boundaries of the township. The lake was renamed Gorman's Lake.

As the business grew, Julia found it increasingly hard to cater to the guests. The place was full of large, cigar-smoking business men from Toronto who drank bootlegged swill well into the night, laughing, talking loudly, occasionally calling each other sons of bitches, which Julia did not want the young Irene to hear.

During the off-season, which lasted only as long as the ice was on the lake, Michael would pace back and forth and wrestle with the demons that Julia thought he should have left in France. One day in the early spring when Irene was six, Julia saw her staring out the window to the lake and eased up behind her to see what she was looking at.

"You know, Mommy," she said without turning around, "I love this lake more than I love you."

It was a childish thing to say, and Julia might well have shrugged it off, but that evening she had the first of her fainting spells when a mist as grey as stone suddenly descended on her, sapping all her strength and energy. She knew at that point that the war between the dream and reality was coming to a close, and that she would eventually have to surrender.

Four for a Boy

"It's as plain as black and white."

"Black and white," Michael repeated. "Black and white." The image of the magpies from the wood three days before popped into his mind. *Thieving magpies*, he thought. What had they stolen? His best friend—where had they taken him? Maybe to hell with most of his brigade.

Michael Gorman's mind raced in wild directions. What was left of his squad—all two of them—had been sent to reserve after the assault. In a single day, the enemy had collapsed. "Run home, you bastards," he'd called after the Germans, shooting them in their backs.

He left his pair of fledgling charges parked under a large, shady elm at the edge of a farm and told them to take cover behind the stone wall of the ruined barn. He straightened his gear and headed back to where the trenches had been. They were now on the edge of a little village called Choulnes, eight miles from where they had started, and where the rail line they followed turned south past twisted metal heaps that had been farmer's sheds or small factories.

Across what had been the no man's land, he saw figures bending over the bodies and dragging carts through the heavy mud. They were black men dressed in khaki. Canadians. A white officer stood and watched the detail with his arms crossed.

"I'm looking for my friend," Gorman called to the officer, a lieutenant who stood propped on an upside-down Enfield, the bayonet still fixed. He was smoking a cigarette.

"Looking for a friend, are you? Mostly former friends here now."

Gorman felt a bile inside him at the officer's flippancy.

Sensing Michael was on the edge of rage, the officer changed his tone as he uprooted the rifle, took another drag from the cigarette. Michael came close and began to whisper so only the officer could hear. "If you lost your right arm, sir, what would your left arm do?" The officer didn't understand the riddle or the metaphor and glanced to make sure that Gorman had both arms.

"We're almost cleaned up here," the lieutenant nodded toward the wagons as he blew a puff of smoke that the wind carried directly into Michael's face.

"I was leading six squad, and seven squad was on my left. We took that nest up there, but seven squad disappeared into the fire. I'm looking for my friend, Sergeant Michael Philips."

"Didn't pick up any sergeants, but you're welcome to see who's on board," he pointed toward the cart that was being hauled away and flicked the end of his dead cigarette into a small pool of red-brown liquid that had gathered in a grenade hole where it hissed and cussed against its fate. Gorman saluted and moved away toward the cart. For an instant, he was relieved, but then remembered that he and Philips were sergeants in name only, that their ranks were noted in the field diary of a lieutenant who had disappeared in a mortar barrage.

Gorman approached the cart. It was a jumble of arms and legs. One hand reached out to him. It was limp and waving with the bumps and jars of the muddy earth, as if it was motioning to him. As Gorman approached, he realized that it belonged to Michael Philips.

"As long as I live," he said quietly, "I cannot take your hand."

And as he walked east to rejoin the remnants of his squad, Gorman stopped for a few moments to rest himself in the afternoon heat. Tall clouds billowed among the shattered poplars as if the trees would poke them and deflate them and make them fall as broken bodies to earth; but earth was no place for the likes of heaven. He saw some birds rising from the open fields. Higher and higher they rose into the air as if they would touch the sun. They did not cheer him. He stood up and donned his gear, slinging his Enfield strap over his shoulder because it was now the only friend left to him in the world. He shook with anger, fatigue, and grief. And as he stepped forward through the scrub to make his way back to the makeshift road that was now filled with men pouring toward the former German line like blood through an artery that was suddenly open and bleeding, he twisted his left foot on something that lay on the ground. He looked down. It was a dead magpie. He bent and lifted the lifeless bird from the mud and, spreading its wings, tossed it in the air to make it fly and give it back to the sky above. It fell to earth and lay there.

One for sorrow, he thought.

❧

With the tinkling of spoons on glasses, the great room that overlooked the lake was alive with the music of a spring that refused to come. The white light reflecting off the snow seemed stark against the laughter of the crowd that had gathered in Sunday suits to celebrate the christening. A man shouted, "Attention everyone, Michael has something to say." A hush fell on the room.

"When I was a child growing up in the city, my father, who was a stationer and a Warwickshire man, used to recite a little rhyme he'd learned as a boy in the fields, hills, and forests he loved. It was an old augury verse through which he said he could predict the future and tell the fortune of the moment."

Someone in the crowded room coughed and Irene patted her new son's bottom. Michael threw a loving glance over to his daughter and his grandchild.

Michael continued, his glass poised in his right hand, "The rhyme went something like this:"

One for sorrow
Two for joy
Three for a girl
Four for a boy
Five for silver
Six for gold
And seven for a secret
Never to be told.

"Now, living in Warwickshire my father must have seen a lot of magpies." He paused for a moment and cleared his throat. "When I was over in France during the last tilt, I saw scores of them. Always wanted to count them and say the little rhyme to myself. Magpies have it good, in their own way. Being both black and white, I suspect they live in a world of grey where they make of it what they will. You've all heard of *The Thieving Magpie?* Who wrote that?"

There was a moment of silence until someone shouted "Rossini!"

Michael laughed, "You can see I'm not an opera buff. When I was in England on furlough during the last war, I went up to my father's old hometown. No one knew me there, but I wandered those fields my father had loved as a boy, and all I saw were magpies! Of course, I wanted to count them by sixes and let everything turn to gold. You know how I love to turn everything to gold." Everyone applauded.

"My friends, that is for us to do in our hearts. That's where the gold is. We live in a time of war, but the miracle is that we also live in a time of love." He paused again and began to shake slightly and stutter, almost distracted. "Hu-hu-how do you tell the future when you see dozens upon dozens of magpies, I ask you? I remember looking from the train carriage window as the towns and farms rolled by and seeing flock after flock. One minute I felt sorrow. The next I thought I was going to be the richest man in the world." The faces in front of him looked confused. Michael recovered quickly. "I just want to let the two of you know that you shouldn't count your magpies before they hatch, even if you become the richest man in the world, Robert." The young couple hugged and smiled.

"We are here today because this is a four magpie day. We celebrate a boy, a beautiful boy, born of love in a world that needs more of it."

Everyone applauded. "Irene," he said, turning to his daughter, "I've gone on long enough with this christening toast, and I think I'm rambling now. When you and Robert went off on your honeymoon last Christmas, I had a strange dream. I dreamt that I was walking through dense brush, just like this place was when we first arrived here. I parted the thick branches that obscured my path, and I saw the lake as it was in those days before we built this lodge. In the lake I saw my reflection, not as I was then or as I am now, but as an old man who was looking up from the depths. And above the still, calm waters, I saw magpies winging through the air—two, four—it doesn't really matter how many.

And I woke up at that instant, and I knew I was going to have a grandson. And here, today, he is cradled in his mother's arms."

The gathering applauded.

"As I stand here today with all of you gathered about me in the hall of this lodge that has brought us so many happy times together, I am proud to offer my blessing and to celebrate my new grandson, Michael Philip Robert McLaughlin, on his christening." He turned to the baby. "It is a helluva world to be born into kid, and some days you'll feel like you're walking on thin ice. But you come into a world where you are loved, and that will always save you. I love what keeps us afloat. My new grandson comes into a world that is, at best, uncertain. We shortly have to depart to drive the proud papa down to Union Station where he will rejoin his squadron. Robert, home on leave from the Air Force, will be going from us tonight to serve Canada in the skies over Britain, France, and, I hope, Germany." A cheer went up. "And I hope you will join me in wishing him and all our beautiful, brave boys courage, strength, and a safe return from the conflict."

"Here! Here!" everyone shouted and toasted. Michael put up his free hand to hush the assembled and continued.

"Robert, I went over there more than twenty years ago. You are going into a world that is only held together by our faith, gumption, and determination to see the conflict through to victory, and by God we shall see victory! As I stand here today, I wish my wife Julia could have been here to see how happy our daughter is…" His voice broke. He paused for a moment and swallowed as the tears welled in his eyes. "Together we had the best of times, and together we weathered the worst of times."

Irene moved through the gathering and came to her father's side.

"But now," Michael continued, "we have a new life and a great deal of hope. This is a two-magpie day! Would you please join me in a toast to the newest member of our family, Michael Phillip Robert McLaughlin, my grandson."

❧

The room was a washed out yellow, the colour of margarine, and the frosted white windows cast a pale light on those within, but left everything beyond to the imagination—the noisy school playground next door, the large pines ringing the hospital.

"I wish I could see the world," Julia said to Irene.

"Yes, I hate these windows, too."

"Not the windows—they're just blind eyes on this place. The doctors can't seem to see what's wrong with me. One doctor says heart. Another says exhaustion. What I meant was that I never got to see the *world*."

"I'm sorry it has been hard."

"Sweetheart," said Julia with a soft smile on her face, "they never tell you it is going to be hard. That's why you do it. You throw your lot in with someone because something in your heart says you must, and because love always seems bigger than anything you can imagine that might go wrong, and even after it is no longer sensible to do so, you still love him because love has longevity and after a while you can't live without it. If that makes any sense. I don't know. And if it doesn't, it will someday. You can't live without what you've grown accustomed to loving."

Julia shifted and wanted to sit up more.

"I mean, it must have been hard for you in the early days," said Irene with sympathy and with a desire to get her mother to share with her the stories that she seemed to keep bottled up inside about how Magpie Point had come into being. Her father had always been brimful, after a scotch or two, about the paradise he had found and how it had given him new life when he thought the entire world had gone dead. "It was all I had to love," he'd said as he shook a finger at Irene, warning her that she needed something to love and hold on to if she was to survive in the world.

"You had me!" Julia had scolded him. "You had me. I helped you cut the logs for this lodge. I was on the other end of the saw, even when I was pregnant. I didn't just keep house, I built the damned place!" She ran off, sobbing, to one of the numbered guest rooms on the upper floor of the great pine lodge.

Julia stared long and hard at the frosted glass window of the hospital room. "Pierce and Carruthers and those men loaned us the money to build the place, which we paid back in no time, but they also thought they owned it, or at least they behaved like they owned it. It was hard. The parties would go on all night, and then they'd be up early, barely able to stand upright, and want to go fishing. That was fine for your father. He'd slept through a war. But I'd be up making them breakfast. The ruckus years didn't last long, though. The crash came, they lost all their money. Then we became a family resort, the lake fished out. A man from town couldn't get rid of a huge mound of sand he'd taken out of an old dune in the corner of his field, so for thirty dollars, which was a lot in those days, your father had it dumped at the edge of the lake so the little ones could walk out and paddle. It was idyllic in its own strange ways. We hired girls to work in the dining room. I had to watch them, and then go and check the rooms and make sure the maids had done their jobs in the mornings. Everything had to be clean as a whistle. The one spot in the day I had was in the midafternoon, in the heat. Up in the room we had that faced away from the lake, I would lie there and listen to those damned cicadas and think, *when will the summer end.* I'm sorry, sweetheart. I'm rambling." Julia closed her eyes. The past had been exhausting.

"Mom," Irene said quietly, in a pleading voice, "I've met a boy. Don't be mad. He works at the resort." Julia opened her eyes slowly.

"You know the rules. We have to be strict about the rules. That is your duty."

"But Mom, he's serious with me. His name is Robert."

"I know the one. I see everything."

"Since we closed down for the season, he's been driving up on the weekends from Toronto to see me. He's at the university, and he wants to go into business when he's through."

"Don't spoil your heart and don't give it easily. There are people in this world who will take everything from you, and they are often the people who come the closest to you. Don't trust what you can't hold on to. You don't know where things are going. You'd think that by 1938 they'd have everything sorted out, but they haven't. I lived through the war. I saw my girlfriends weeping, and lives and hopes shattered, one by one. They became the women who occupy the single seats at the back of the dining room. Do you know that California vase on the table in the great room, the glass globe with the yellow rose? They say it will last forever because someone dipped a California rose in wax and then suspended it in alcohol. Forever is a lie. The best you can do is to protect yourself."

Irene left the hospital after her mother dozed off and walked quietly with tears rolling down her cheeks along the main street of the small town. Men looked up from the doorways of the hardware store and the barber shop and probably wanted to ask her why she was crying, but everyone in the town knew her mother was ill and was going to die. But Irene was not crying for her mother but for the forevers she wanted—the husband, the children, the life that would always assure her there would be a tomorrow. Forever was the rocks and the trees upon which her father had built their lives. That was what she believed in.

※

As Michael, Irene, Robert, and the baby reached Union Station, the flyers were assembling into their units in the great hall. High around the cornice of the structure were the names of the destinations a train could take a person: from Moncton in the east to Vancouver in the west—Fort William, Regina, Moose Jaw, North Bay in large carved uncials etched in the flesh-coloured stone. It felt strange to Irene that none of them said "Overseas" or "Forever." Robert grabbed Irene, kissed her, saluted his father-in-law, and with the other men from his command, proceeded in step down the tunnel corridor. Michael and Irene followed the men to the platform where people, many in tears, were waving handkerchiefs and calling after the boys to write, to look after themselves, to come home safe. Irene kissed the top of her baby's small, round, bald head and whispered, "There goes your daddy," as the train pulled away.

In the crowded station, Michael Gorman caught sight of someone he seemed to recognize. *I mustn't let Maggie recognize me*, he thought. *Not now. I can't speak to her now.*

On the return drive north, Irene lay in the back seat, the baby nestled in blankets in a basket on the floor. Michael thought she was asleep.

"Dad?"

"Yes, dear?"

"There was a woman on the platform tonight, and she looked as if she recognized you. Did you see her?"

"No, sweet, I didn't see anyone. The only person in my mind was Robert."

Irene was silent for a long time. Michael heard her weeping. "I feel as if he's been stolen from me."

Michael wanted to pull the car over to console her, but instead he fell silent. After a long period, thinking she might be asleep, he said in a low voice, almost as if he knew he was lying to her, "He'll return, don't worry."

Three months later a telegram arrived at the lodge regretting to inform the eighteen year-old Mrs. Robert McLaughlin that her husband, Flight Lt. Robert Wentworth McLaughlin RCAF was missing in action.

Five for Silver

By the time Irene purchased the last piece of property on what was now known as Gorman's Lake, her hair had changed from a

63

soft nutty brown to a defiant, shining helmet of steel. In regional real-estate circles she was known as "the warrior" for her fierce determination to turn property into money.

With her husband's life insurance policy, she had invested wisely in the post-war housing boom that had taken place in the city. Then there had been the McLaughlin family inheritance, which was sizeable; Robert had come from a city family that had admirably survived the crash of '29 and invested its money in failing machine plants that, in turn, served the war industries. She'd bought up run-down farms on the outskirts of the city, and flipped them to developers while maintaining a piece of the final home sales. Even the government had helped. The Veterans' Bill had given each fighting man a choice on his return: a university education, a start in a business, or a piece of land with a home on it. Irene had made a fortune on the latter. Bobby Jr. would want for nothing.

Her father still oversaw the Magpie Point lodge operations, but he was slowing considerably. The lodge was still turning a profit, but the high-end customers from the financial circles of the city had now purchased their own weekend places on nearby lakes. Irene had had a piece of that action as well, as their real-estate agent.

In the late fifties she'd married another land dealer, Ricky de Soto, who had come to the city from the States and had made his own fortune in industrial properties. Ricky met Irene at a resort managers' convention in Philadelphia. She liked the way he held his cigarette both in his lips and in his fingers. His pencil thin moustache added an element of the movie star to his appearance, though he was a noticeable two inches shorter than Irene and slightly overweight. His cream-coloured jackets and his slicked-back black hair looked tidy. He had avoided the war by jumping back and forth across the border in various occupations. When he arrived at Magpie Point for the first time, he stood out like a sore thumb.

Ricky had no time for young Robert. "Hey kid, you live at a resort, go have a vacation or something," he would say to the boy when the child came to him with a ball and glove or with a game. "I ain't your father." In the winters, Ricky would take Irene away to Miami Beach to show her what a real resort was like. Bobby would sit in the silent great hall of the resort with his grandfather, who would hide behind a newspaper. From time to time, Michael would suddenly slam the paper down and go to the window to weep. He would weep in front of the child, but in front of no one else. At first Bobby was frightened of the sobbing, grey-haired man, his shoulders heaving, his fingers pressing against his eyes and his head bowed, but gradually Bobby came to feel nothing.

The years of the fifties passed at Magpie Point like sun beams slowly settling in an empty room. The worlds in the photographs of favoured patrons that hung on the walls of the dining hall slowly faded from black and white to greyish yellow, only to be replaced by new colour prints that gradually faded to the blue of a smoky sky. The veterans, now educated and married, flocked to the lake with their families. The Gormans had never had it so good, except for Ricky, who would pace back and forth on the sun deck or in the great hall and make people nervous as he puffed at his cigarette. He always seemed to be waiting for word of something that never arrived.

One night, Irene got a telephone call from the provincial police and was told that Ricky had driven headlong into an oncoming truck after stopping for a nightcap on his way north from Buffalo. Before he left, he had not had the heart to tell her that he owed a large gambling debt to some men from New York and that he was going to Buffalo to pay it off with what was not his, namely the resort. Had he actually gone to the meeting, rather than miss it to stare at Niagara Falls from the American side for several hours, Magpie Point would have been lost.

That had been in the early sixties, and she often wondered how young Bobby dealt with the shock of losing two fathers in his short life. As closely as she could see, Bobby adjusted well. He spent his summers at the lodge and made friends, if only for a week or two, with the children who came to stay. Temporary playmates were better than no playmates at all.

The lodge now catered to families, and Irene sought to expand the business by looking at the long-term investment. Those families, she calculated, would someday want to retire to a lakeside community, and she was determined to make Gorman's Lake their destination. Along the shoreline of the once peaceful bay, Irene built numerous cottages that she rented out each summer, upgrading and improving services during the winter, and employing many of the locals who had given up hardscrabble farming for trades. Eventually, she was elected mayor of the township, and using her political weight, brought the highway within a mile of the lake just before the old railway was abandoned to the scrub growth and sickly pines.

※

When he was old enough, Bobby Jr. was sent to one of the finest boarding schools in Toronto, where his wealth and his mother's power in what was now known as cottage country placed him in the "in-crowd." For his sixteenth birthday, Irene bought him a long, silver run-about with a huge, overpowered Evinrude at the stern. On summer nights, Bobby and his friends would break the stillness racing from one island to another. He was always surrounded by a king's court of guests and had the run of "his pond." If he didn't like what another teenager said or did, especially if they were a guest at the lodge, Bobby could tell them off and muscle them out. It was, he told them, his lake by name and ownership. Irene had worried that the boat would lead to trouble, but she was more afraid of it flipping over and drowning him or catching fire with him on board. Two summers later, when Bobby was almost the age she had been when his father had been shot down, the trouble began.

There was a girl named Sheila Menczuski who worked at the lodge. She set breakfast in the early morning, joined the maids to clean rooms at midmorning, and then waited on the luncheon crowd until her break, during which she'd usually lay on a cot to catch some sun on the staff deck off to the side of the central building. Sheila was tall and blond. Her ambition was to become a dentist, and as she lay on the sun-cot, she would read her science books for the coming year. She was determined not to live the life she had known in the lower east end of the city, where her father worked in a tire factory. One day she looked up from her physiology book and saw Bobby standing in front of her.

"Hey, good looking, want to come for a ride in my boat?"

"I prefer older men," she replied, dropping her sunglasses down her nose and looking the young Mr. McLaughlin up and down. He was standing in front of her, his body eclipsing the sun, leaving only a halo of late afternoon light filtering through the arms of the tall pines.

"Good things come in young packages," he replied.

"I think that's 'small packages.'"

"I'm not small," he said, grinning at her. "I can show you some of the most beautiful places on the lake tonight. Come by the dock at eleven."

Sheila went back to her book, but as she stared at the text and graphs and diagrams, the image of the sun through the trees and the light around the young man's body stirred in her. *This could be mine*, she thought as she looked over the rail of the employee deck at the sunlight as it shattered into jewels on the surface of the lake. She made up her mind that she would take the boat ride that evening.

As the motorboat roared through the night, and her blond hair flowed like a river of silver in the wind, Shelia decided that this was all anyone could want—the lake, the trees, the dark, calming waters that caught the reflection of the stars.

❧

The Humber's waters were calm and gave the impression that time would stand still. The dip of his paddle in the brown depths of the river raised little silver droplets that jumped in the light. Maggie lay on the bottom of the canoe with her head propped on a cushion that rested against Michael Philips' back. Michael Gorman sat in the aft, steering gently because he was the better canoeist and because he wanted to watch Maggie as the sunlight fell on her face. Her auburn hair flowed around her shoulders and onto the white of the billows of her sleeves. She opened her right eye slightly, squinting gently in the sun, and as she looked at Gorman, a small smile appeared on her face.

He glanced to his left as Maggie shut her eyes again. The remains of the old mill stood in the distance, its stone façade a strange and lonely ruin that spoke from an age far older than it actually was, as if the river, draped in the green veil of weeping willows trailing their long tendrils into the flow, had been there since the mists of time had cleared and the first knights went to challenge their dragons in an eternal test of wits.

He, too, closed his eyes to listen to the stillness of the river and sat his paddle on the runnel to let the craft drift. He thought back to that church social in the garden of Julia's parents' Rosedale home. Everyone had said to him, "Michael Gorman, you are a lucky son of a gun that Julia fancies you. And she is so far above your station, you must be coming up in the world." Whenever he heard something like that, he knew he would have to marry Julia, though it made him feel that he was less than the man he knew he was. Her father had said, "Mr. Gorman, you are going to have to raise yourself up for her," and Michael knew that the course of his life would be spent fulfilling that demand. But in that instant, as he stood there considering the gentleman of means he would have to become to earn the right to Julia's hand, he looked up and met the eyes he would never be able to put from his mind. Beneath the Japanese lanterns and the spreading arms of a huge stately elm, the young woman approached and volunteered to clear some of the dishes from the tables that had been set with strawberry desserts and lemon-yellow cakes. And that was when he and Maggie met. Courteously, he extended his hand, and she hers, and they said nothing until Michael Phillips sidled up and said, "This is Maggie Calmon. I was introduced to her earlier, and now I pass on that pleasure. Maggie, this is Michael Gorman, my friend since childhood." And he added, as if a voice out of nowhere, distant and instant, "You are going to keep paddling, aren't you?"

Philips turned and glanced over his shoulder at Gorman who corrected his course and steered north to where the river bent slightly to the west and vanished into mystery among the trees.

"We'll have to bottle this afternoon and take it with us," he said.

"Don't talk of that now," Maggie replied in almost a whisper as her arm listlessly reached over the runnel of the canoe as if it thirsted for the touch of the cool current. Gorman raised his paddle as she cupped her hand and let the silver drops fall into her palm. Michael Philips had talked of the great adventure that lay ahead, but all Michael Gorman felt in his heart was a great emptying.

"There will always be days like this," he said to his two companions, Maggie and her betrothed, Michael Philips, "but this one is certainly ours, ours forever. Let's make it last."

❧

Irene sat staring at the strange, hunched man with large broad hands who sat opposite her in the leather armchair.

"Mr. Menczuski," she said emphatically, "there is absolutely no proof that my son is the father of your daughter's child. You are making a very rash claim."

"My daughter Sheila," he said, gripping his hat, his hands tightening in a rage he struggled to control, "was an employee of yours last summer, and your son took advantage of her. Now she has to leave university. Your son forced himself on her and brought dishonour to our family. I am here to tell you that if you do not co-operate with me, I will make a scandal out of this. I have learned from some of the locals here that you are planning to run for Parliament in the next election. I am here to demand that you do me honour or I will ..."

"Or you will what, Mr. Menczuski? Are you blackmailing me? Because I can assure you that I will report this matter to the police if you are threatening my family or my reputation in any way."

"Mrs. de Soto, you misunderstand me. I want your son to honour my daughter by marrying her."

"That is out of the question. The boy isn't twenty yet, he's not marrying the daughter of a factory worker, and there is no proof that he is the father of the child."

"Boys do not share such information with their mothers. I spoke to my daughter."

"I am offended by your accusation, and I think you should leave." Irene rose and opened the door. Sheila's father shuffled out, looking back in disgust and uttering something incomprehensible. Michael descended the grand staircase and paused on the bottom step as the man rushed by, his cheeks red with rage.

"I want to speak with Bobby immediately," she snorted at her father.

"Bobby said he was going ice fishing. He's out there on the lake," Michael said pointing out the window. "He left shortly after that gentleman showed up."

"Ice fishing? No one has caught anything in years out there."

Michael and Irene went into the dining room and stared through the large picture window that looked out over the late March scene. The world looked dead and grey. The wind had grown still and not a sound could be heard. In the distance they saw the outline of a hunched, dark figure walking across the ice toward one of the hump-backed stone islands. But between him and the outcrop lay a steel-brown patch that was not covered by snow. And in an instant the trudging figure vanished through the ice.

Six for Gold

One November evening about a decade after Bobby's death, Michael and Irene were at their apartment overlooking the valley on St. Clair. They were at their city condo to look after some business matters when they received a call from the town works commissioner.

"The lodge is gone," he said.

"What's gone?" demanded Irene as her father suddenly woke from an evening snooze in an armchair.

"The lodge," he repeated. "It burned earlier this evening right down to the foundations. I'm glad I'm speaking to you because I know the news would shatter your father. He put his life into that place. I'm sorry to tell you it's gone. I hope you can break it to him gently."

"Gone," Irene repeated. "I see." She put down the receiver. The lifetime of work her father and her mother had put into the place, building it from a potato farm in the bush into a thriving business, only to see it decline into a decrepit ghost: it was all gone now. She thought of the years she had grown up there, the mahogany launches lined up at the pier to refuel, the men in white shirts and cream summer flannels, the women in their floral dresses and big hats, the golden sunsets that she saw out her bedroom window each summer night that turned the colours of gasoline on water. Her son on the lake in his silver run-about flashed through her mind. She pictured her mother directing the kitchen staff, showing them exactly how the food should be prepared. She saw her mother, arms crossed, standing at the sideboard at the front of the dining room, inspecting the diners as the meal progressed, circulating among them to make sure everything was all right. She remembered Bobby as a little boy running across the lawn toward the small, sandy beach that had been built along the lake. She pictured him as a four year old climbing the staircase and turning to look at her as she sent him to bed, and the image reached out to her saying, "Come. Come with me."

"Gone," she said, turning to her father and offering only a single word. "The lodge is gone." Michael pulled himself up in his chair and sat silently, staring straight ahead as if not taking in the news. In his mind he was moving slowly through the foggy wood, his bayonet fixed and his heart leaping in fright.

"The problem with paradises," Julia had said, "is that they always fall." In that instant she and Michael had been sitting in the sad little farmhouse, eating their boiled potatoes. "You're a dreamer," she said, "and do you know what dreamers are? They are people who steal the heart from reality. They are thieves, magpies who don't care what they put in their nest as long as it is shiny and bright."

Michael looked at Irene. He nodded. "Yes, I understand." He paused. "Was anyone hurt?"

Irene shook her head. "I don't know. I didn't ask. I can call Bud back and find out."

Michael nodded again. "That would make me feel better. We have to take a roll call." She stared at him incredulously. "Find out, would you, how many are left and fit for duty." After a long silence, Irene turned to look out the window, plotting her next move. Michael sat with his head still bowed as if a verdict had been passed on him.

When the snows melted away from the blackened beams and twisted electrical wires that had triggered the fire, Michael stared at the ruins of his lodge and discovered that there was, indeed, something left.

Among the jumble of charred and fallen beams that felt so familiar, he found the picture of the Humber River still hanging on the wall where he had nailed it in 1927, when the main lodge opened. The picture had darkened, but Michael spit on the tips of his fingers and rubbed the cracked glass until the scene emerged. The river, he thought, had been a deeper blue, and he wanted to look away from the scene because something told him that its depths could not be sounded. In the litter of what had been the basement, he found the pump-head from the old farmhouse that he had saved as a souvenir of Julia's hardships in the early days. Michael caught the toe of his shoe on an object that almost seemed to be reaching to hold him, but this time he refused to look down for fear that it might have wings.

He asked Irene what they should do. Should they rebuild? Could they put it back the way it had been? But she had shaken her head at the old man, saying nothing as if she thought he could not hear her. She unrolled some papers from a large blue cardboard tube and spread them before him on the apartment's kitchen table. She pointed at an artist's rendering of tall, thin rows of grey wooden townhouses. On the balcony of one, a couple with silver hair pointed toward a marina and a small horizon of open water. They were tanned and healthy and smiling.

"This is what we're going to do: retirement condominiums. One of them will be yours. This is the way of the future." Soon the trees were torn down. True to her word, the townhouses crowded shoulder to shoulder, ringing the bay on both sides. Where the balconies overlooked the lake, the new marina took shape. A sign on the driveway in from the main road read:

Welcome to
Magpie Point Retirement Paradise
On
Gorman's Lake
Another Fine Corvidae Property

❧

The two Michaels sat down together on the hull of a felled poplar that had been left behind when the sappers came through just ahead of them to strip the brush for their new assembly point and to establish new communication trenches. There was a heavy scent of smoke and the sulphur reek of cordite about the two men. They held their tunics over the small cooking fire and watched as the lice leapt like stray kernels of popcorn from the khaki cloth to the flames.

Gorman stood up and urinated into a cloth he kept in his kit for polishing his buttons. Philips did the same.

"Spit and polish," Philips said with a wry grin.

"Make 'em shine for the officers. It is all piss on something or someone," Gorman laughed. They began going over and over the brass buttons that ran down the fronts of their uniforms, polishing the beaver, its garland of maple leafs, and the crown above it, until it all began to shine like gold.

Gorman stared at the image on the fastener. "I'll wager that sucker lives in a quiet wood, somewhere beautiful and peaceful where the loons call and there's a morning mist just hovering over the waters that are still as tea in a dead man's cup."

"That's poetic of you. It's just a button."

"No, Mike, I see it as if it's a fortune teller's glass ball, as if it's a dream."

"That's a nice dream to have."

"Well, there it is," said Gorman holding up the uniform at arm's length so he could imagine what an inspecting officer might see. "A little piece of paradise bright enough to pass muster."

❧

Late one June evening, Michael Gorman went and stood at the end of the pier that jutted from the new marina into the lake.

He stood there with his hands in his pockets, his gaze turning from the sky to the lake to the townhouses that lined the shore. The first evening lights were lit in the windows. The lake waters at the end of the pier smelled strongly of gasoline and rainbow swirls of fuel rose and fell with the subtle motion of the water. He looked across the stillness that spread before him to see if the loons would appear around the outer arm of the bay. But the lake was empty. The loons had been gone for more than forty years, yet he had not realized they were missing until now.

He felt a stone gnaw at the pit of his stomach and it sickened him. "What have I done? Oh my God, what have I done? What have I stolen from God's good earth?" he whispered to himself. Steadying himself on a light standard, he leaned over and looked deeply into his reflection on the dark waters of the lake; for a moment he thought he saw what he had been looking for since the day he parted the bushes and caught his first glimpse of paradise.

And Seven for a Secret Never to Be Told

"My friends, we are gathered here today to pay our last respects to a man who came to this lake with his bride in search of a dream, so many years ago. As we stand here by the shores of the waters that bear his name and prepare to scatter his ashes upon those waters, we can remind ourselves that this country was made by individuals such as Michael Gorman who lived their lives according to the strength of their vision. Look around you. I see here, today, the faces of so many people from this community whose lives were changed for the better because Michael Gorman was here to offer employment and opportunity to a developing region. I see here, today, his daughter Irene, with whom he overcame so many of life's challenges with dignity, courage, and a desire for progress. Here was a man who despite adversity reached out and constantly seized opportunity." The minister paused in his eulogy and gave a reassuring nod to Irene.

Within a few minutes, Michael Gorman's ashes were spread upon the wind, which picked them up and carried them across the water toward the hump-backed island where the pines spread their branches in the setting sun. Irene and the other mourners made their way to the end of the pier, where she turned and greeted each one, thanking them for coming and remembering her father. One mourner, a grey-haired man in his seventies, stopped and pressed an envelope into Irene's hands.

"Do I know you?" she asked. "Were you a friend of my father's?"

He held her hand for a moment. "Well, I guess you could say I knew your father, although I would have liked to have known him better. He changed my life. I've put it all in the letter. I have to go now, but you can read it later when things settle down, and if you want you can call me." With that, the man disappeared into the crowd.

That night, Irene sat in her condo with the sliding door open and, with the first mosquitoes and black flies buzzing at the screen, slid off her shoes, put on her reading glasses, and opened the letter.

Dear Mrs. de Soto:

Perhaps I should call you Irene, but at the moment you might think that forward of me. I wanted to write and tell you what a profound effect your father had on my life. I don't know how to tell you this, and I guess there is no indirect way of saying this, but I am your brother.

My name is John Philips. My mother, the late Margaret Philips, was married to your father's war buddy, Michael Philips. I don't know whether your father ever spoke of my mother or of my father. All I have is what my mother told me. They had been buddies before the war, enlisted together, and served together throughout what I've been told was the worst of it.

Throughout my childhood, your father would come to visit our home. He would give my mother money to clothe me and look after my needs. My mother would never allow me to meet him directly. I used to watch him out the front window of my childhood home in downtown Toronto. He would stop and turn around as he left and stare at the house. I would watch him, and he saw me many times, and we simply stared at each other, a bit like a bird and a bird watcher sizing each other up. His visits were frequent though they were brief. I wish we had known each other. I feel as if that portion of my life was stolen from me.

When I was a teenager, I found a telephone number lying on the small table in our front hall. It was for somewhere far outside the city and had his name scrawled across it. I called him, but it must have been someone else who answered, another man, because he said Michael Gorman wasn't there at the moment and that he was always busy and couldn't be reached. I wrote to him, though. He kept a postbox in Toronto, and he always wrote back. I treasure his letters because they were full of good advice and encouragement for me. He often told me stories about my father, Michael Philips, and their war experiences together. He looked after his friend, especially toward the end of the war. Michael Philips was killed at the Battle of Arras, so I never knew him. I was born just after he and your father left. I still have my mother's letters from him telling me how good your father was to him, how many times he had saved his life. I suppose in that war, they both saved each other's lives. In any case, your father's letters were words to grow by.

I remember that once my mother and I were very sick, and your father brought a doctor to the house, and then dropped off a nurse who was there at our bedside, along with a cook and housekeeper until we got through the worst of it. We didn't seem to have enough on our own, and I don't know what my mother lived on. She sold a farm her husband had left her when I was a small boy, but I always suspected that the money from that ran out before I was out of grade school. We never wanted for anything, which was strange, and she always bought me new clothes to wear after your father had dropped by. It didn't take me long to put two and two together. Your father, bless him, supported us. I once confronted my mother about this, and she said that Michael Gorman—the first time I heard your father's full name—had been an old friend of my father's and had promised to look after me. I thought it was the gesture of a great man, like something out of Great Expectations or something.

When I needed extra money for university after the war (I went through on the Veteran's Bill), it was your father who helped me out and sent me what I needed. I became a businessman in Kitchener, failed at a few things I'd tried to do, and retired recently on a small pension I'd managed to put together for myself and my wife. I figured it was time to quit while I was ahead and enjoy what I have.

When Mom was dying in the hospital several years ago, she told me the story of who I am. She shared the secret of my parentage with me. She told me that she and your father had secretly been lovers in the weeks before the enlistment of the two Michaels, even though she had promised herself to Michael Philips. She told me Michael Gorman was my father.

As I said, at the time I felt my past had been stolen from me, that the man who came to visit should have had the decency to be a dad to me. I remember reading about your lodge, the wonderful summers that people spent there. I looked you up and almost came to visit your father at one point, but I stopped short at the end of your road when I saw the beautiful place that had been Michael Gorman's home. I couldn't bring myself to enter that world. In his defense, he probably had his reasons for keeping me in my own world apart from his. He was probably trying to look after you and your mom.

All I am asking for from you is friendship. It might be too much to ask to be considered family, to be brought into the flock. I suppose it is hard to admit a new person into one's life: they bring with them their joys and their sorrows, and it is hard for others to embrace those. I guess I am asking for your bravery.

In any case, I hope you will keep in touch with me, perhaps meet with me and my wife, and maybe even become part of our family. I have enclosed my phone number, and I look forward to speaking with you and getting to know more about who I really am. If you should decide not to contact me, I would understand."

Sincerely,
John Michael Philips

Irene looked at the letter for a long time, holding it in her hands and staring out the window into the night. She folded it over and tore it up into tiny pieces, threw it in the waste can, and then wept quietly to herself on the couch. *No*, she thought to herself, *secrets do not need to be told or shared.* She had no reason to change her life now.

She rose and went to the window as a cool breeze drifted in and a full moon appeared between the clouds and reflected in the lake. She sensed that it was the same wind that had carried her father's ashes that afternoon, that he was there on that breeze. But she slammed the sliding door shut, shook off the night air as if it was a passing chill, turned out the lights, and went to bed. Her last thoughts as she fell asleep were about the strange circumstances of her father's death.

Michael Gorman had been found floating in the lake that bore his name. The coroner who examined his body assumed that he had simply slipped from the dock, fallen in the cold water, and lost his heart rhythm as a result of the sudden shock. His death had been ruled accidental.

But if the truth be known, Michael Gorman's death was not caused by an accidental slip into the lake. As he bent over and stared at his reflection in the water on that June evening, he did see something that he knew he could reach, and it was there in the depths where he always suspected it lay. Was it a lake, shining in the morning light as he parted the pines sixty years before? Was it the sorrowful body of a dead bird half buried in the mud that he would lift up in the hope that it would fly again? Was it the first thin veneer of winter ice that he would scoop gently from the still surface on a windless grey day, as if he could hold back the winter? The truth of the matter is that no one knows. Beneath the public and even the private person, there is another life, one that speaks only in the depths of the heart, and at that, so rarely. He leaned gently from the dock and slipped into the water. At first it stung his body, but gradually he felt at ease in it, as if every sinew in his flesh was part of what was around him. He swam deeper and deeper, and as he looked up he could see the golden sky gradually disappearing above him and another light ahead of him reaching out for him. And he loved what he saw because it took him back to a moment in time when he had been happy, a moment that had been stolen from him by circumstances and obligations and the fires of time. He reached out and for an instant he held it.

It was a summer evening. As he strolled along the maple-lined streets of the city, a soft, warm breeze tossed his hair across his forehead. His right arm was crooked so that it could be taken by the person next to him, and his hand rested upon his stomach. The gentle hand of the woman beside him pulled him to a stop, and she reached up and brushed the lock from his brow.

"Michael Gorman, you are the one I love. Being with you is like walking in Eden." And he bent down to the small, auburn-haired woman, and, putting a kiss on the end of his finger, pressed it gently, as if hushing her, to Maggie's lips.

States of Claude

Sketch

There are several things you should know about Old Masters etchings. The poet Auden said "About suffering they were never wrong, The Old Masters: how well they understood its human position …" and this might be true except that not all the Old Masters depicted suffering. Some, such as Jacques Callot, did so exceptionally, but others simply wanted to remember what is beautiful and mysterious in the emotional currents of life and to celebrate those moments of infinite reflection. Look at the updraft of wind on a summer morning as your train slides through the green pasture lands of southern Ontario and you will see the simplicity, the haunted majesty that inhabits the works of my favourite artist, Claude Lorrain.

What I love about etchings, especially those by Lorrain, is that a single pull from a press that marks a moment in time is living evidence of growth, evolution, and aging. And always the etching will tell you that its life, the life in the plate that the artist has carved with the care and strength of his own hands, is slowly ebbing away each time ink touches paper to create a newer yet ever older image. I look in a mirror every morning as I shave my aged face, and I feel relieved in many ways that my final state is approaching, that point when my image will no longer leave an impression upon the blank sheet of the world. Every etching reminds me of my own frailty and the beautiful yet limited humanity of those I have loved.

An etching begins with a pencil sketch, a few pale lines reflecting the shape of what the artist takes from the world and puts upon the page. Artists such as Claude would venture into the fields and forests of a very different Europe from the one I knew and almost despised, and accompanied by memory and imagination, wait for that moment when the world would speak to them in either a soft caress to the back of the neck—the warmth of a lover's hand—or by startling them with the ferocity of life's grim realities. The sublime. The surprise. The touch of warmth. The unending summer day. The pitiless storm. The road not yet travelled. From those few pale pencil lines upon a sheet, began the life of a work of art that eventually had to run its course in a series of impressions or states until the plate, the bones of the living thing, simply faded to a faint whisper of an image that could not be uttered again.

I began collecting Claude almost by accident. During the final days of the war, as my unit moved through Holland, I took shelter from enemy fire in the remains of an old house—its library, to be exact. I sat with my back propped against one of the few remaining walls as a shell exploded on the other side. A picture hanging directly above me came crashing down on my helmet, its glass shattering, the frame coming undone from the mat, the picture falling into my hands from its anchoring.

The picture, an old etching, was a scene of a summer day beside a river. A group of children were dancing in a meadow, and the trees appeared to bend and sway around their tiny figures in time to an invisible music that blew through the monochrome light and shadow. I brushed the shards of glass from my uniform and stared at the scene. I liked it immediately. In fact, I fell in love with it. I had seen such a moment in a dream shortly after my unit landed in Normandy, and it was a vision that clarified for me the reason I was fighting in that awful war. I wanted to dance with those children beside that river. I rolled up the etching and tucked it in my rucksack. It would become a map for the rest of my life.

First State

The first state of an etching is often incomplete. Artists such as Dürer would test their central images before adding necessary pieces of the background. I once purchased an etching by the Dutchman Antonie Waterloo that shows a cart on a road. The driver is prodding his horse with the painful persuasion of a whip. Neither cart nor horse is going anywhere. What I loved about the etching was that the wheels were missing. The artist hadn't cut them in yet with his burin, the sharp instrument that etchers use to impose their lines on copper plates. That is the absurd proposition of the first state. They remind me of that line from Paul's Letter to the Hebrews about "the possibility of things hoped for and the evidence of things not seen." Such images are portraits of what is to come, echoes of what will be, and presences of possibilities—in short, they are acts of faith.

Yet whatever the deficiencies of an incomplete image, there is something pristine, clean, and newborn about the first state. And there are artists such as Claude who almost never left a first state unfinished. He didn't set his plates to ink without knowing, instinctively, that everything that should be there was there. First state Claudes are worth a king's ransom, and it is usually kings and queens who collect them. I once lost out on one at an auction in Chicago on a snowy night. Had I gone a hundred dollars higher in the bidding, I might have possessed something so prized that it would have made my other etchings pale in comparison. A first state's lines are precise and clean, yet show the flaws of the plate itself hidden within the image, flaws that the artist himself could not have foreseen. They are beautiful because after the limited first printing the cleaned plate will never have the same clarity, the same sense of innocence, the same desire to be perfect, to please those who behold it.

Following the war, I was offered a posting with the Ministry of Foreign Affairs that was, in those days, known as the Foreign Ministry. I am Anglo-Irish Canadian by descent, but I think myself French by nature and passion. I was offered, perhaps as a result of decorated war service, the job of assistant undersecretary for Cultural Affairs in Paris. It was an interesting job. I had the opportunity to work with a group of unusual people, including my superior, a man called Armitage. I tried to have as little to do with them as possible. Paris was as it more or less had always been, though Europe was a ruin around it. I busied myself by shuttling around musicians and actors who were touring France in order to promote Canadian arts, or the lack of them. But on the days when I was not on embassy duty, I haunted the bookstalls and print shops and antique markets, wandering through the maze of forgotten things in the north end and thumbing through baskets of old artworks in the makeshift stands along the Seine. That is where I found my next several Claudes and where I met Sophie Gravure. Her grandfather owned the stand as well as a small print shop on Rue Racine just down from the National Theatre. He had grown too arthritic during what he called the "unheated" years of the war, so he took to the shop and left the stand to his protégé. Under her tutelage, my love of Claude grew. So did my love of Sophie Gravure.

As a new member of the diplomatic corps, my learning curve was steep. Guy Dufour, the ambassador, called me into his office. Sitting beside him was Sir William Stephenson, who I would later learn was not merely an industrial genius, but the man who was code-named Intrepid during and after the war, the spymaster of the free world.

"To what I do owe this honour?" I said, extending my hand to the august captain of industry and then to Monsieur Dufour.

"Have a seat, Monsieur Page. We have something very serious to discuss with you. The mission, we believe, has been infiltrated by at least one Communist spy, possibly two. We know your record. We have investigated you thoroughly, or should I say the Americans have investigated you thoroughly."

"Damned Americans," said Stephenson. "Have their hands in everything these days."

Dufour nodded and continued. "We are not sure who it is. We are asking you to help us ferret out the spy. It is a matter of major secrecy and poses a considerable risk to the mission here and to all of us who are not Communists, to say nothing of the nation we represent."

I was given instructions on what to watch for—secret meetings, telephone calls that are picked up after a certain number of unanswered rings, the familiar faces of my co-workers appearing in out of the way café windows, and such things. I was intrigued. This was slightly better than greeting fat sopranos and tenors at the airport. I agreed to do what I could. I also realized, as I returned to my desk, that my frequent visits to the print shop on Rue Racine and my acquisitions of Sophie's unmarked, brown paper packages at the quayside might be construed as suspicious behavior.

So, who was it? Who was the spy? Renard, the communications officer? He had access to all the information that came in and went out. He had the codes. He knew the system. Was Armitage in on it? I was never quite sure what Armitage did and his title was shady enough as protocol officer to leave me wondering if it was him. There was Paquette who oversaw matters of passports and emergencies among visiting Canadian nationals. He was in a perfect situation for comings and goings and midnight meetings. And the longer I thought about it, frankly, the less I cared. I was more concerned with how I would go about pursuing my passion for Claudes. They were, in the post-war years, becoming more and more expensive by the week—though in comparison to what they are worth today in the auction houses and elite London galleries near Saville Row, I have to laugh. Someone, though, might ask where I got the money for these delicacies and question, in a philistine way, why any sane grown man would fall in love to the degree I had with etchings by a single artist and a few of his contemporaries thrown in for good measure.

I made one last trip, in broad daylight on a Saturday morning, to Monsieur Stylaut's shop near the National Theatre. Sophie was there. We had all become friends because of my habit. "I have been told by my embassy to be careful of my movements and my actions. I can't say why," I explained.

"Ah," said Monsieur Stylaut, "the wiles of diplomacy. I understand." Sophie's face fell.

"But we can continue our business relationship another way," I said.

Sophie smiled and said, "I can deliver the prints of your choice to your apartment, no? Leave it to me."

Several nights later, a knock came to my apartment door around midnight. My first thought was *No, they aren't going to bring me in for questioning, are they?* But when I opened the door, there stood Sophie with a long baguette sticking out of a brown paper bag. "I do not think I was followed," she said wryly as she stepped in and laid the bread on a table in the corner of the room. "Voila!" She pulled a knife from her pocket, brandished it in the air, and then pointed it at my neck.

"Are you going to kill me?" I asked.

"No. I am going to feed you, body and soul."

When the loaf came out of the paper bag, I noticed it had a cut around its circumference. Sophie pulled off the end, and inside the loaf she had several prints rolled up in cellophane. My first thought was *This is going to make me look even more suspicious.*

"What is the knife for?"

"To cut the bread, of course."

She sliced off a piece and held it to my lips. I stared into her eyes. She turned aside in a flash and unrolled the prints. The one that immediately caught my eye and stole my heart was *Round Tower with Shooting Fireworks*. "This one," I said as if I had made a major choice in my life.

"It looks like a man in love," smiled Sophie. "It looks like …"

I turned and looked into her eyes, took her in my arms, and kissed her. The print was still on the table with the bread the next morning as I made us both café au lait. We broke off pieces of the baguette and fed them to each other.

We became entangled in each other's lives and the life of a world that had grown paranoid and cold. The lines of what constituted reality were no longer sharp and delineated. The innocent first state was leaving my life, and I could do nothing about it except try to hold on to the fresh and beautiful image of Sophie's brown eyes.

Second State

The round tower appears in about eighty percent of Claude's paintings and in about sixty percent of his etchings. In his early work the tower is round and strong. It always reminds me of those Martello towers one sees in Kingston and Quebec City, round fortifications built on the orders of the Duke of Wellington to defend an under-garrisoned, innocent country against invasions from America or France. James Joyce lived in one such tower just south of Dublin and opens his novel *Ulysses* there. In the forties in Canada one could not simply go out and buy a copy of *Ulysses* to read. It was against the law. It would be burned by the authorities. This bothered me because I had lost friends fighting to keep books out of the flames. At the time, I did not realize that the forces of philistinism were rampant all over the free world. I am a snob, and to me snobbery comes from skill, vision, and knowledge. It is a desire to know something more than the reality of this life and is the hallmark of a truly free society. I thought of myself as that tower standing on the heights or the rocks or at the end of the long road, a symbol of defiance against the forces of stupidity in the universe.

John Keats wrote of Claude's tower in one of his poems, and I would stand by Keats any day against those who use the guise of blind patriotism to either hide their wrong-doings or to espouse a mentality of dull-headedness that allows individuals to be manipulated by evil men and women. Keats declared:

> *You know the Enchanted Castle—it doth stand*
> *Upon a rock, on the border of a lake,*
> *Nested in trees, which all do seem to shake*
> *From some old magic-like Urganda's sword.*
> *O Phoebus! that I had thy sacred word*
> *To show this castle, in fair dreaming wise,*
> *Unto my friend, while sick and ill he lies!*

I wanted nothing more than to show it to Sophie, but it was she who showed it to me.

The round tower that Claude is said to have used as the model for his tower is the tomb of a wealthy Roman noble woman, Caecilia Metella. The structure is located on the Via Appia Antica, on the way to and from Rome, a place in between places, a landmark that says the perfection of the eternal city is not far off. In most of Claude's works, it is there for decorative purposes, but my hunch (and I am purely an amateur art historian) is that the tower is a metaphor for Claude himself. He is La Tour, stalwart, the will to live in a world teeming with life, a container for the timeless dead, and a landmark for travellers. He is the essence of a work of art. In his youth, the tower is often distant, but as he grows older, and his works become more regretful and often darker, the tower is besieged, and eventually it is broken open, its heart laid bare by the storms of life in etchings such as *Tempest with a Shipwreck*. A beautiful galleon, of the kind that fascinated Auden in the same poem where he talked about suffering and the Old Masters, is dashed upon rocks as the tower crumbles above it. Entropy rules nature. One should not reject it. Without the storms, there would be no joy, and joy is what I found with Sophie. The metaphorical tower was always somewhere in the distance, sometimes right beside us, as our relationship intensified and blossomed into love. She called me *La Tour*. A man in love is rarely one to look over his shoulder, and I very quickly forgot about spying on my colleagues.

I consider the days I fell in love with Sophie to have been my second state. The second state of an etching is the complete and correct state. More often than not, the second state is signed; the artist is satisfied, and he is ready to share with the world what he has done. Yet for all its perfection, there is the sense that something original and raw has been lost.

One Saturday she sent me a message telling me to meet her early the next morning at the Gare du Nord. I had no idea what she had planned. I met her at the station, and she presented me with my ticket. "We are going to Lorraine," she said. Claude's original name was not Lorrain. In reality he was Claude Gellée, the third of five sons of a family who lived in the duchy of Lorraine, a part of France comprised of pasture lands and gently rolling landscapes that border Germany and Belgium. He was orphaned, as was Sophie, early in his teenage years. He was a naturally gifted artist, and when his skills at draftsmanship and painting exceeded those of his teachers in France, he travelled to Italy to learn more and to practice his craft among the very best in the world. There, because of the excellence of his art, he became known as "the Lorraine" or simply Claude Lorrain. Lorraine is an area through which armies have passed for centuries, wreaking their havoc on the populace, but leaving the indomitable landscape untouched for the most part, as Claude would have seen it in the seventeenth century.

Sophie had a wicker basket slung over her arm. It was covered in a red and white check cloth and had, of course, a long baguette protruding from the top of it like the arm of someone waving for help. All the way to our remote rural destination, she pointed out the spires of ancient churches and towns until what we saw out the carriage window became green and timeless and beautiful in the June morning. The dew had left the grasses and crops glistening, and an updraft through the leaves made the trees sway gently as if they were dancing to an unheard music.

We disembarked at the small station of Saint Nicolas de Myre, which to me was in the middle of nowhere. Cattle were lowing and in the distance we heard goats bleating. It was as if I had walked into one of Claude's etchings. "Do you know this St. Nicolas?" asked Sophie.

"As in Merry Christmas?"

"Exactly."

"Why here?" I questioned.

"A knight of Lorraine, centuries and centuries ago, was part of the guard that transported the remains of the saint from Greece to Italy, and he managed to sneak out the bone of his little finger and bring it to Lorraine. It resided in the church in Saint Nicolas de Myre. That's why it is always Christmas here."

"And what is my present, ma petite Mère Noël?"

"Be patient. The picture is not yet complete."

I took her arm as we laughed. We walked along a forest pathway for what seemed at least a kilometer and found ourselves in a copse that opened into a small meadow by a stream. Sophie pulled a broad blue cloth from her basket and spread it on the ground. "You are now a dweller by the thicket," she said, "the thicket of de Myre." To my surprise, Sophie not only spread out lunch on plates but also took out a small wind-up record player and an aged 78rpm recording of Johann Heinrich Schmelzer's Sonata IV. "Let us dance," she said, "just like in that story you told me about your first Claude."

"Will we be under fire just like then?"

"I certainly hope not. We will be under the trees, under the sky, and maybe under the watchful eyes of children who wish to dance with us."

And as we danced to the lilt of the scratchy record, a group of children and farm men and women did emerge from the coppice and laughed at the two fools from Paris cavorting in the country-side. The sunlight sparkled in Sophie's eyes. The long blond hair of a young girl who came to dance with us lit up as if her head was haloed with eternal summer.

We spun round and round and the leaves on the trees blew in the warm air just as they are in that moment of sunlit perfection in so many Claudes. When the music stopped, I held Sophie close to me and felt her heart beating against mine, her breath heavy and full of summer on my cheek, and the sensation of life, vivid life, in every sinew of my being. The dream had become a reality. Art had become life. I had fought the war for all the obvious reasons, and for this secret reason: to make this rare and beautiful moment live forever.

And somewhere in the back of my mind I thought I heard Claude speaking to me from the gently rolling pastures of Lorraine, telling me that when art reaches perfection, there is no boundary between it and life. There is only life.

That evening on the train back to Paris as Sophie cuddled against me, her cheek resting on the shoulder of my soft Donegal tweed, and the pale outline of her face illumined by a full summer moon, I asked her to spend her life with me, and she whispered the one word that inhabits all great dreams, *Yes.*

Third State

But even the leaves on those beautiful trees where we danced beside the flowing river had to drop when their season ran its course, except in Claude's etchings. The moment made a lasting impression on me, but the more I try to recall it in my mind, the more it darkens until the lines and outlines of everything fade into a silence of vision that settles on my mind like nightfall.

This is the third state. In most of Claude's third states he palimpsests his signature, not because he disowns the image or the plate, but because he cannot bear to admit by way of his name that he has lost that beautiful perfection that was and never can be again. Some of Claude's imitators, his epigoni, try to recreate the moment when art triumphs over time. There was Richard Earlom, the English mezzotint engraver, whose work can be gently excused because it is not really Claude at all, but Earlom experimenting in a rather beautiful homage to Gellée. Armand Durand, the nineteenth-century copyist who did so much to try to share Claude's art by imitating his achievements in exacting copy, line by line, simply watered the value of those original images by creating shadows of states that in detail are true to the original, but in spirit are soul-less. He managed to flood the market with his copies—Claude's for everyone!—and made it difficult for collectors and the uninitiated to tell the difference between what is real and what is less than Claude.

The only way you can truly tell a genuine Claude from a later imitator such as Durand or Léon Gaucherel is to hold the paper up to the light to see the watermark that lies at the heart of a print. Van Gelder paper has been produced and used for centuries by great artists. Whistler haunted second-hand bookshops in London and Paris in search of old volumes that had been printed on early Van Gelder paper. He would purchase the volumes, whatever the cost, simply for the purpose of removing the blank pages from the last signature of a folio or quarto, and upon those blank sheets he would print his own masterpieces. True Claudes, when light passes through their paper, reveal markings such as a heart with a cross on top, the symbol of love and service and martyrdom. Another familiar watermark is that of a putti or an angel, standing tip-toed upon the top of the world: a secret, surprise statement that art is the link between heaven and earth.

The final etching of Claude's long career, an image he produced in his early eighties, is a gentle piece titled *The Goatherd*. But the fact that they are goats rather than his usual sheep suggests that his vision of the world ended not in comedy but in tragedy, in the ancient Greek sense of *tragos oides*, the goat song. The tower is there, but it is set off in the distance to the left of the plate, as if watching the gentle passing of time in the shade of a large, spreading oak tree. A goatherd, perhaps Pan himself, is sitting in the shadows, filling the forest with the music of his pipes, though even in the first impression he is hard to discern. By the time the etching arrives at its third impression, the image has all but paled out. The goatherd is not playing his pipes, but resting his chin pensively on his hand, which is in turn resting on his cocked knee. His back is turned to a narrow foot bridge where two people, possibly lovers, are making their way toward the cluster of buildings and the tower, perhaps to seek refuge from a dying nature—but the reality is that they are frozen in time and they never arrive. A broad plain of ocean stretches infinitely behind him.

One night in our Toronto apartment, many years after our Paris experience, Sophie woke me to tell me she was having difficulty breathing. I called an ambulance to rush her to the hospital. Holding her hand as she lay on the stretcher in the elevator, I realized that the walls were covered in mirrors, and the two of us stretched infinitely, state after state, impression after impression to that point where time and perspective become infinite.

As they put the oxygen mask over Sophie's face, there was so much I wanted to tell her. I wanted to tell her everything I'd kept secret. I wanted to tell her who the mole in the embassy really was. It was not Dufour as she suspected. Though at the height of the Cold War, when the hearings in Washington were ruining the lives of so many, he'd leapt one morning from the upper window of the embassy, narrowly missing a woman with a pram on the boulevard below.

Nor was it Renard, though he'd made a point of flaunting his wish to be a mole to anyone in the diplomatic corps that might listen. Perhaps he knew more than he let on, perhaps being the soggy bon vivant of late night conversation with people not worth talking to was his way of playing the game.

As much as I pretended not to pay attention to the question of espionage around me, and as much as I was a man in love at the time, distracted by the beauty of a woman who was a work of art, it was I who fingered Armitage, and Armitage who fingered me. In the end, a committee of back benchers from rural constituencies believed me over Armitage. So, I suppose, in a way, I have answered the question about how I managed to finance my extravagance at a time when positions in the Foreign Service afforded little in the way of compensation other than patriotic pride.

I was spying for the French.

Armitage, I later discovered, was slipping information to the British.

There were people in both the French and the British embassies that I recruited to work for us Canadians. I enjoyed that. Those were the rules of the game. One was not supposed to take it all too seriously. We fed each other rubbish information in the way that cheap print dealers tried to sell me fake Dürers printed on nineteenth-century paper towels. Looking back on it, I can't see what use any of the information was. We were all on the same side, and I considered it just a form of friendliness. Only those who were not playing the game properly, and I mean those who were trading real Cold War secrets that could lead to the obliteration of millions of people, took things seriously. They were the ones who leapt from the upper-story windows. Their burden of information was far too weighty to permit them to dance the dance. That was not for me. It was then that espionage ceased to be an art and became about the destruction of life and beauty and art.

There are few things in this world that are worth betraying one's country for, namely love and beauty and the ability to convey ideas and aspirations that are genuinely human across borders of time and politics. And if there is a flaw in the story of Claude, a story that I often mistake in my mind for my own story, it is that the life of his art was as short lived and perishable as the loaves of bread that transported his etchings to me under Sophie's arm. I suppose we have to be prepared to carry love and beauty beyond even those perishing commodities that convey our values through time.

Claude's plates disappeared shortly after his death in 1682, and they were missing for more than one hundred and fifty years until a diligent English art collector and publisher by the name of William McCreery unearthed them in Italy just as Napoleon's troops were ransacking the tombs of ancient Romans and laying waste to the tower of Caecilia Metella—a place they mistook for a fortified position not unlike a Martello tower. McCreery raced home to London with the precious pieces of copper and the images they cradled, dodging the French navy off the coast of Spain, and riding a post stage to London from Portsmouth as if he were carrying urgent news. He was. He cleaned the residue of ancient, congealed ink from Claude's plates, printing a limited portfolio edition using those delicately etched original surfaces. I can imagine him standing there as each was pulled from the press, the light shining through the Van Gelder watermark, the chiaroscuro of black lines re-emerging and speaking again after their long sleep, filling him with reverence for the artist. These are what I call the fourth state of Claude. They are without the imperfections of the first state printings, yet they are an expression of resurrection, a testimony that there can be life after death, that the grave can open and a lost summer day can shine over us again as beautiful as the moment time forsook it. These fourth states possess the character and clarity of the second state images, and the whispering delicacy of the third state. They are the final voice of the wind moving through those landscapes of leafy trees.

And in an instant of divine insight into the beauty and meaning and sad reality of art, McCreery realized that the greatest sin he could commit would be to allow Claude's work to escape its realm of privilege and rarity. As a tribute to the artist and as a way of releasing the spirit held within the image, McCreery printed off about twenty or so of each image then melted down the plates for scrap. I can almost see them glowing with the wind in the boughs of the trees, the dancers looking into each other's eyes one last time, and the proud and resolute tower staring down the final storm of death as they dissolved into the heated crucible from which they had once been born.

The copper, one legend has it, ended up as surgical tools that would help to heal the wounds of a world that was being torn apart by a war of thanatotic rage. Or the copper became roofing for a gallery or the dome of a repaired cathedral, perhaps even the sheathing for the House of Commons. Or it is lurking in plates of etchings carved by Whistler or Haden later in the century, when the art of etching was reborn by those who saw the importance of distinguishing between light and darkness. In their green-orange lustre, the world of the heart, the eye, and the imagination was preserved, to be repeated over and over like the reflection of two old and frightened lovers caught between mirrors in a cramped and almost airless elevator, holding hands forever on the way to the reality of our inevitable state.

The Dragon Cloth

Miss Reid looked anxious as she stood in the front room of the smoky apartment. She peered through the beaded curtains that hung between her and the next mysterious room, where a gathering of men threw glares at her and spoke amongst themselves in Cantonese. The air was filled with the pungent odour of tobacco mixed with a lilt of incense. It took her breath away. She cleared her throat in what was an act of self-resuscitation as much as an expression of nervousness. *Courage*, she thought to herself. *This is how things begin.* The beads parted and a woman bowed before her as she shuffled a little girl into place.

"My daughter," said the woman, her hair pulled tightly into a braid that hung down the back of a shimmering, greenish-yellow embroidered silk jacket. With a note of tentativeness she repeated herself, "My daughter, Li Fan Yi."

The little girl looked frightened and apprehensive as she made her cautious entrance, throwing a furtive glance back at the steely eyed men and then at her mother. Miss Reid held her hand out to the child. "It is very good to meet you Li Fan Yi." The girl did not take her hand. The child's eyes grew wide, and she pulled on her raw silk tunic as if preparing herself for an appearance on stage.

"Li Fanny," Miss Reid said, kneeling to look the little girl in the eyes. The child nodded with recognition. "You don't know any English yet, do you?" The child stared into the woman's face. "You don't know any English yet, but I shall teach you. I shall start by calling you by your English name. Henceforth, to me and to all who speak English you shall be Fanny Lee." Miss Reid held out both hands to Fanny as she said her name, and gradually the child trusted her and took them. The child repeated the words, "Fanny Lee." Miss Reid nodded.

"Yes, Fanny Lee. Good. I think you'll do wonderfully well." She stood up and nodded to the mother who nodded back. "Good day," she offered. The mother simply smiled and bowed, and smiled and bowed again as the teacher and pupil made their exit and disappeared down the long, dark staircase into the ramshackle streets of Toronto's Chinatown. The little girl did not look back.

Miss Reid learned that much of the Chinese community in Toronto lived in an enclave of shacks and squattered huts behind the registry office. The pillars of the classical temple where Toronto kept its memory rose up beside the broken-down dwellings that had been hideous since the middle of the previous century. The streets, if they could be called that, were little more than mud paths that reeked of sewage and rotten food. The life span of a child born into Chinatown, a doctor at the church had told her, was less than six months. The buildings were unheated in the winter, and in summer swarms of flies crawled on the few panes of rippled glass that had not broken under the weight of the years. A policeman who patrolled the perimeter of the Chinese parts, as they were known, often stopped her. "You don't want to go in there miss, not a fine woman such as yourself."

But she did go in every Sunday to see if she could convince the children to come to church so she could teach them English. The world that the young faces came from was a terrible weight around their necks, but English, Miss Reid believed, was an equalizer.

Before long, Miss Reid had joined up with the other teacher, Miss Monkman. Margaret Monkman was a seamstress by trade who worked in the backrooms of the Eaton's ladies wear department. Together, they devised a strategy for bringing the children to their church. They would make them uniforms. Miss Monkman found several bolts of white raw silk that the department manager wanted to throw away because of a slight flaw in the weave. For the boys, they fashioned small jackets with two buttons on the front, each one piped in a different colour ribbon so they would feel unique. The girls were each given small dresses of the same material, also with the piping in a personal colour. Fanny Lee's piping was purple.

Together the women, Miss Monkman led by Miss Reid, would make their way into Chinatown each Sunday to collect the boys and girls and bring them to the Presbyterian church. On the steps of the granite edifice, a phalanx of elders stood with their arms crossed and stern, stone looks of inspection on their whiskered faces.

For heaven's sake, thought Miss Reid, *they'll scare the children.* She understood just how skeptical the elders were. After all, it had taken considerable persuasion for them to even allow Chinese people into the church. Such things were not done. They were heathen. But that had been exactly Miss Reid's striking point as she conspired with Reverend Patterson, a broad-brogued Irishman who saw the potential in the Bible classes. They had seen the poverty of Chinatown, the solemn funeral processions of weeping mothers dressed in white, the colour of mourning, as they followed their children's coffins to the burial grounds. They had put the proposition to a meeting of the elders: let us teach the Gospel by teaching them English. Reverend Patterson, the persuasive son of a Roscommon horse-trader, had pushed his luck and won. The children's session on Sunday afternoons was to be followed by an evening gathering of the Bachelor's society. The Bachelors were the hundred or more Chinese men who lived in the city and had not been able to raise the punishing head tax to bring wives from China.

As the children entered the church, Fanny let go of Miss Reid's hand. She stopped and stood in front of the elders who peered down at her as if she were an exhibit under glass. She bowed theatrically to them as she announced, "Fanny Lee."

Red was a lucky colour, as Miss Reid came to understand. It was the colour of prosperity and happiness. That was why the room was painted red. The porcelain tea service with its tiny cups was spread out on a red and gold cloth on the table before her. The mothers sat around the edges of the room smiling and nodding at her. A red envelope with her name printed neatly on it lay in front of her.

One of the women peered around the corner through the beaded curtain and summoned the little girls into the room. Each was carrying with them a small package done up in string and red sealing wax. The children lined up in front of Miss Reid, some solemn and some giggling. Fanny held out her package first.

"This is something that we have made with our mothers for you," she said proudly to her teacher, each word pronounced with precision and the hint of an English accent. It was a correctness that made her the envy of the class and the chief object of pride among her family.

Carefully peeling the red wax seal from the paper to preserve the embossed characters, Miss Reid undid the red paper, looking up at the girls who showed growing expectation on their faces. Inside the red paper was a folded green cloth that the teacher stretched out before her on the tea table. In the centre of the cloth, a green and gold dragon with eyes as blue as heaven reared up from a sea of jade-coloured silk. From its mouth spouted a lick of red, blue, orange, and yellow flames. It was surrounded by a circular key-work design in rich umber and shining ruby that was, in turn, embellished beyond its borders with celestial images of stars and flowers blooming in bright yellow and vibrant orange. Miss Reid stared at the gift and gasped in amazement.

She had learned a great deal from her students: they'd taught her the profound and beautiful meaning of the fine designs they embroidered with their mothers. The dragon had the head of a camel, the horns of a deer, the eyes of a rabbit, the ears of a cow, the neck of a snake, the belly of a frog, the scales of a fish, the claws of a hawk, and the paws of a tiger. It had the downy wings of an eaglet, and appeared to beat the cosmos as it struggled to take its first flight through a green heaven, a flight that would let it soar beyond a world where such creatures were chained and condemned to caves and nightmares. All animals seemed assembled in the dragon—it was the sum of all beasts, a symbol for the world itself. It took her breath away as it seemed to draw its own breath. In that instant, she felt that she saw what centuries of Chinese people had seen in the mythical beast—not the menace slain by ancient saints, but the very essence of the world that could be if it were contained within a single word and spoken in a whisper. The dragon, especially a green one with blue eyes, was a symbol of heaven, a benevolent protector of health and fortune, and a harbinger of future prosperity,

"Oh, it is absolutely beautiful!" she exclaimed as the girls and their mothers broke into applause. "This is the most beautiful thing in my entire trousseau. I shall treasure it always!"

"Miss Reid," Fanny announced, "we are sorry that you will be leaving us to marry Mr. Miller, but we all want you to have something with you from our hearts as you journey through your life. You gave us all something from your heart when you taught us to recite the Bible and gave us the gift of English. We are all older now, and we are going to school. Mae has decided to become a doctor because you encouraged her to learn the parts of the body in the Song of Solomon. Her little brother, Billy, wants to become a soldier because you taught him the story of King David and how he overcame the giant Goliath. And you taught me the story of Salome and John the Baptist, and I dream of becoming an actress."

Indeed Miss Reid remembered Fanny's stage debut during one of the Sunday morning services, when the class had performed its recitations in front of the congregation. As the faithful looked on, the children had stood in the chancel with their hands clasped and their eyes focused on the assembly. Some had made costumes out of foil and paper bags, some out of old sacks and some had simply stood in their raw silk tunics. But Fanny had raided her mother's jade for rings and had appeared just moments before the service dressed in an elaborate skirt. She had transformed herself into Salome, and when her turn arrived she began to dance.

Scowls appeared on the faces of the older parishioners, the stern elders who considered high kicks and leaps, or any form of dancing, a sacrilege. Reverend Patterson's face turned red as he tried to restrain his laughter—he already had his answer for the sin-seers in an Old Testament verse that would remind them that David, the King of Israel, had danced naked before his people, although not in a Presbyterian church. The tension of that moment was broken by Fanny's last kick. As her leg came down, so did the large bloomers she'd donned underneath her skirt. With a great guffaw, Reverend Patterson leapt to his feet and applauded as Fanny covered for her costume problem by kicking the bloomers into the air and catching them as she bent into her bow.

The moment was quieted when Reverend Patterson offered a blessing on the beautiful children. He commended them on their fine effort and asked God to guide them on the path of righteous learning as they pursued their dreams of mastering the language through which the Lord spoke to each and every one of them on Sunday.

The trousseau tea ended with the little girls crying tears that were of joy and of sadness over the departure of their teacher. They promised that they would all keep in touch with each other, that the girls would tell their teacher how their studies were progressing, and the teacher would tell them about the joys of married life and her new home.

As she spread the dragon cloth on her bed that evening, Miss Reid examined the careful stitching, the gentle shimmer of the green silk, and the shape of the dragon rearing up in defiance of all obstacles. She sat down to compose thank-you letters to each of them for their wonderful gifts and especially for the beautiful dragon cloth. And she thought to herself, *Yes, they will succeed.*

MARCH 20, 1921

Dear Miss Reid, or should I say Mrs. Miller. (I will always think of you as my Miss Reid and I hope you will always think of me as Fanny Lee.)

It has been two long years since you left to become a married woman, and I hope you are very happy in your new home with your husband. I dream someday of finding someone I can love and spend my entire life with. You reminded me in your last letter that such a day would, indeed, come, and I know you are always certain that our dreams will come true. I look forward to that day and take strength from your faith in our ability to control our own destiny.

I am writing with great sadness. My father, a man who was very respected in our community, has passed away. As a mayor of Chinatown, he had a very grand funeral, and a dragon danced at the head of his procession to ward off any evil spirits that might stand in the way of his path to the afterlife. As a Christian, I do not believe in evil spirits, but told my mother that if the dragon would make her happy then it should dance a way clear toward the reward my father had worked so hard to attain.

He had come to Canada in the 1870s (I guess he was a very old man when he passed away, although neither my mother nor I knew his exact age). He had worked on the railway as a labourer and had made his way east where he used the money he had saved to start a small store here in Toronto for other members of the community. As the community grew he became wealthier until he was able to pay the head tax and bring a bride, my mother, from China. When he was dying, he told me that Canada was a gold mountain, that it was a place where, as legend had it, a man might fill his coat and hat with all the riches of the world. He certainly filled his hat and his coat, I told him, but my father reminded me that that same man might lose those riches on the long swim home across the ocean.

When my father died my mother came to me in tears. She told me that it had been his last request that my mother and I return to China with his bones, so that he may be buried in the centre of the world. As his dutiful daughter, I must fulfill his last request and spend my life in China. I do not feel that China is my home. I have grown to love the language that you taught me, its poets and its beautiful books. I feel as if I must now wander lonely as a cloud, never catching a glimpse of the host of golden daffodils. My mother and I will be leaving tomorrow, but I shall write to you when I am in China, and I will tell you of what I learn there.

With love and best wishes, I remain your ever-faithful student, Fanny Lee.

❧

Mrs. Miller gazed at the envelope. The letter had taken three days to come. Tears welled in her eyes because she had not been there to see her pupil off. Fanny was almost a young woman now, and China would be unfamiliar to her. Perhaps whenever and wherever she arrived, she could put Fanny in touch with one of the local missionaries there and find her work as a teacher. But that was for later. For the moment, all she felt in her heart was emptiness and a sadness that stretched across the sky and over the sea like a strange, smoky plume blown by the clouds.

JULY 16, 1932

Dear Mrs. Miller:

I hope this letter reaches you and finds you well. I still have the address that you gave me, the one for your new home. I wanted to write to you and tell you what has become of me. I had meant to write to you sooner, but life in China came as a total shock to me and it took a very long time for me to adjust to the ways and customs here. When I arrived, I realized I was no longer a Canadian, but I also realized that I was not Chinese. I felt lost between two worlds like a piece of bamboo open at both ends. The women here seem bound to custom. They may dream, but they are not allowed to live those dreams. But I decided that my life would be different, even if I had to defy everything that my relatives told me I must be.

I had always dreamt of going to university, but that never came to be. Women here are not allowed to go to university unless they are from very rich families. We are only moderately well-off. But to be moderately well-off here is to live fairly well, and I have made the most of the opportunities I have been given.

When we arrived in China my mother and I travelled with my father's bones to an estate my uncle had purchased for us on the outskirts of Shanghai. The city is a strange place. It is full of people who are not Chinese. It has far more varieties of nationalities than Toronto. There are White Russians who have fled here because of the fall of the Czar. They keep to themselves and live close to the sea. It is said they all have boats secretly locked away in sheds in case the Red agents come for them in the night.

The Russians purchase the boats from the German Jews who are here. They arrive and claim they are in hiding because there are political forces in their home country that tell them they are not welcome to live there anymore. Everyone seems to be welcome in Shanghai. More and more people every day are coming.

The house that my uncle bought to honour our return is very beautiful. It is outside the crowded streets of the city. There is a British school nearby and most of the people around us are English. I am able to speak to them because of the language you taught me. The estate is splendid. It has an old great house and many servants. It is not cramped like in the inner city, where the Jews and the Chinese residents are crowded into alleyways lined with houses we call shikumen.

With the money my father had made in Toronto, my mother was able to secure tutors for me, and she even built me my own small theatre in our garden with footlights, curtains, and backdrops. I put on plays for my relatives, and often enlisted some of the local children and foreigners from the mission school down the road to assist me in my productions. Every time I stepped on stage, I remembered what you told me about being brave and speaking to the world through my dreams.

It was during a garden production of Othello that I met a young man named Chen Sun Lo, who was a student at the mission school. He is very handsome and very kind. We love to stroll beside the river on an avenue called the Bund that is lined with beautiful buildings—banks, hotels, offices of international firms. Chen always told me he wanted to make movies in Shanghai, and now he is one the most famous producers in all of China and I am his leading lady. We have made eight motion pictures, and he is planning next year to add sound. Not only am I his star, but I am also his lover now.

I hope you are not shocked to hear that I have a lover. In China marriages are difficult. Marriages are arranged by our families. Because my mother was considered a foreigner here, it was very hard for her to make a proper union for me. This was the source of considerable shame for my family, and I have had to put that shame behind me. But I do not feel shame for myself. The life of a movie actress has allowed me to live beyond the boundaries that this society would normally set for me. When people in China see me portray heroines who accomplish great things, I hope they will feel that they too can do the same themselves. I hope they will face their problems and soar above them.

I have learned many things—I even took flying lessons several years ago. I love flying. It reminds me of poetry: the freedom, the liberty to go where my imagination takes me. And as I fly, I look down on the world and all its troubles, and for a few moments I am beyond anyone's grasp. I feel like a word that has been set free by being spoken.

My own dear Miss Reid, I wish that you and I could be together again, if only for an afternoon, to talk about poetry and hope and all the things we dream. I hope that someday my movies will be seen in Canada. Then you will know what has become of me. I had thought of sending you some of the Chinese movie magazines, but as I looked at them I realized you could not read them. Perhaps someday I will teach you to speak Chinese and to read the poetry of this nation. There is beauty here in so many things. I shall spend an entire lifetime trying to learn about this place and who I really am, and even then I shall feel that I have fallen short.

You once told me when I was a little girl that it might be impossible to learn everything, but that we should take what we learn and make something real of it. I hope that I have, and I thank you for showing me what lay beyond that tiny, red-walled apartment in Toronto. I do miss you and I will write again.
Forever your pupil,
Fanny Lee

Mrs. Miller looked at the beautiful letter and then scanned the envelope for a return address. There was so much the two could have shared. Mrs. Miller had watched proudly as little Mae with her anatomy books became the first Chinese female doctor to graduate from the University of Toronto. Some of the boys from the class had also graduated from university and become successful businessmen. She wanted to write to Fanny to tell her how proud she was of all her accomplishments, but Fanny had not written a return address on the envelope. The front of the letter simply bore her own address, a postmark in both English and Chinese from a land far so far away it seemed impossible to imagine, and a cancelled orange stamp in the upper right-hand corner. Mrs. Miller squinted, and beneath the franking she could see the details of a rampant dragon drawing up his claws and challenging the world.

Throughout the summer of 1937, Mrs. Miller read the papers and followed the Japanese invasion of China. The chrysanthemum proved poisonous to the dragon. Shanghai fell after a short battle. It was called the pearl city because of its iridescence in the morning mists. It rose up out of the lowlands and the outer peninsula as if it were a jewel worth dying for—and many did.

The Japanese did not bomb the industries they had established in the city. Instead they bombed the train station, the French area, the British area including the avenues around Fanny's house, and the offices of international companies along the Nanjing road. From the little theatre at the end of her garden where her childhood had taken a bow, Fanny Li watched her city burn. It was not dragon's breath, but the fire of hell that Reverend Patterson had once told them about.

Within a week, the gateway to China, the place where the Yangtze River met the sea, had fallen. There were reports that terrible atrocities had been committed there. A photo taken at the train station of a badly burned baby screaming in pain made its way across the international wire services. The world was growing darker by the day. War was ready to break out in Europe at any time. Miss Reid prayed for Fanny's family and wondered if her pupil had escaped from the city, leaving behind her garden and her theatre. Had Fanny been caught in the invasion? Reports of massive arrests of people involved in the government and universities who had not escaped the onslaught in time became more and more ominous as summer dragged into fall.

Fanny found the baggy clothes the old gardener had left in his house behind the theatre. A small, stooped man, he had bent and grown closer to the earth. His feet never touched shoes, so Fanny decided that she, too, would have to go barefoot if her plan was to work. The mud of the garden was cool and wet and it felt like death between her toes. Her feet were white and her toe nails had been painted red. She found a piece of steel wool and worked the polish off until the ends of her toes were pale and almost ready to bleed. She found some brown grease paint in the theatre's dressing room, a colour she had never used because she'd always played the pale princess in the dramas, the empress who faced enemies without fear. She melted the hardened make-up in a small brass dish propped over a candle, and when she poured it on her feet, the heat stung her to life. She felt the fire rise up inside her as she dirtied her face and cropped her hair short, so that she looked like a boy who had seen too much of the world.

In the street on the outskirts of the British zone, someone had abandoned a cart full of dirty hay, and she strained to pull its weight behind her as she walked toward the Japanese holding camp. Behind the barbed wire she could smell the rancid presence of death, of earth that had soured and filled with blood, and hear the helpless cries of men and women who were screaming for a hope that would not come. She stood at the gate.

※

Late one December afternoon, after she had put away her groceries and sat down for a few minutes to catch her breath before preparing supper for her daughter and her husband, Mrs. Miller opened the evening paper and began to thumb through the stories of a sad world. On page seven, something caught her eye. It was the picture of a Chinese woman, smiling, wearing an aviator's helmet. The headline read "Toronto-Born Actress Frees Husband."

A Toronto-born Chinese actress, Fanny Lee, arrived safely in Sydney yesterday with her movie-producer husband, following her daring jail-break rescue of him from a Japanese prison camp.

Fanny Lee's husband, Lowson Chen, was taken prisoner by Japanese authorities during the fall of Shanghai two months ago. He was sentenced to death by the district commander of Shanghai and was awaiting execution.

Miss Lee told the Australian press yesterday that she disguised herself as a man and fell in with a team of labourers who were returning to the camp from a work detail. Spiriting a loaded revolver in her trousers, Miss Lee located her husband and shot her way out of the camp to where an automobile waited to take the pair to a nearby airfield. Miss Lee then shot her way into the hangar, commandeered a small Japanese military plane, and flew it to the Nationalist lines. During the flight she managed to elude the pursuit of several Japanese fighter planes.

From there, she and Chen made their way to Australia where they held a press conference yesterday.

Chen and Lee told reporters of the atrocities that were taking place in China, and urged the governments of free nations to stand up to the Japanese aggression in their homeland.

Commenting on her escape from enormous perils, an event which outshone any of the famous actress's films, Miss Lee explained that courage is not simply the domain of stories, but something that one has to practice on a daily basis.

Mrs. Miller put down the newspaper and went upstairs to her room. She knelt down beside the cedar chest that contained many of the things from her trousseau. Beneath a nightgown she had worn on her honeymoon, she found a length of purple thread wound up in a ball, and as it slipped from her fingers, it opened like a streamer in a dragon dance parade. She reached into the depths of her precious belongings, took out a package wrapped in red paper, and slowly she unfolded each crease to reveal the dragon cloth. The last light from a dying winter sun caught the shimmer of the silk as it was freed from its cave. The bright colours danced as if the heavens themselves had come alive, and the dragon spread its wings and soared.

Something Close to Brilliance, Something Close to Love

Every night, just before they turned out the lights, they would lie together in the darkness and embrace as best they could around her expanding belly. One of the last things they did before they fell asleep was to talk to the baby. She would tell the baby how much she was loved and stroke the round bump and pat it lovingly and sometimes the baby would kick back. He would put his mouth to his wife's stomach and sing "Somewhere Over the Rainbow" and tell the baby that he was her daddy and that he loved her very much. Often in this ritual, he would tap out rhythmic patterns, and the baby would respond with taps in groups of twos and threes. Without fail, they kept up this line of communication as if the baby was a miner trapped in a dark pit and clinging to the faintest lifeline of hope until the time came for her emergence. The date had been chosen to induce labour. The nursery had been set up, the car seat installed, the stroller studied and unfolded, and the appointment made at St. Gabriel's Hospital to start the ball rolling, as the nurse said when she gave his wife the inducement injection. He pointed out that it was ironic that a date of birth could be chosen legally but not a date of death. The nurse frowned. Dark humour was out of place in a maternity ward.

"This won't take effect for several hours," she said as she disposed of the syringe and helped the mother-to-be into her top.

"Why don't you two do some shopping at the Eaton Centre until it is time to come back."

"That might be too far," his wife said. "I think we'll just stroll up and down Queen Street and maybe grab a sandwich."

Just opposite St. Gabriel's was a kitchen store full of gadgets and glassware and pots and pans. His wife sat down near the front when the man behind the counter said, "Any day now, eh?" and she nodded and replied that it was closer to any minute.

Her husband found a teapot, a nifty little stainless-steel four cupper. As he paid the $14.95 for it, the man behind the counter wished them both good luck with the new one and said, "Take your wife's arm," as he held the door for them. With nowhere else to go for the next few hours, they stepped into a diner opposite the hospital. The husband spotted a former student of his behind the counter.

"What'll it be, prof?" asked the young man. The couple each ordered bacon on a bun with fries and sat down in a booth. The young man brought them the day's *Toronto Star*.

"This is much nicer than last night," he said to her.

"Yes, what was all that about?" she asked.

They'd been out the evening before for a last night of freedom. They'd gone to a movie at a theatre on Eglinton and afterward had nipped into a restaurant for burgers and shakes. On the way to their booth, he'd spotted two spinster high school teachers who had taught him years before—a history teacher with her white hair piled in a bun atop her head, and an aggravating English teacher with steel-grey hair and stern-looking glasses. She had almost ruined English for him. He introduced his wife to the two women. "We're going in so they can induce labour tomorrow," he said. "We're going to have a daughter."

The English teacher raised her eyebrows and pointed to his wife. "How could anyone bring a child into Mike Harris's Ontario?"

He stepped back shocked and nudged his wife away. "Don't let those fools fill you with doubt," his wife said. "We are doing the right thing. We have to believe that."

When it came time to leave the diner, his former student shouted goodbye, and the young man's father came out from behind the counter to hold the door for them. "I hope you have a child like my son. He's a great kid." Father and son shouted good luck to the couple. He took his wife's arm and helped her across a windy, leaf-strewn Queen Street to the admitting entrance. A nurse with a clipboard greeted them in the entrance way, "Right on time. We'll take your wife, and you have to go this way to register her and the child."

The registration process seemed to last forever. Form after form had to be filled in. In attempting the birth registry, he had to drop one of the names they had chosen for the baby. In the end, what was left was still pretty but not quite as long, and there would have to be some explaining to a grandmother whose name would not continue into the next generation.

By the time he was given his wife's room number, it was early evening. He helped her shower and dressed her in her blue open-backed gown and gently eased her back into her bed. The dilation had started and so had the pain. He tried to talk to her, but she told him to be quiet. For a while she stared at a magazine, slowly turning the pages before she handed it over to him. Through a whistle-mouth, she blew air in puffs as they had practised together in the birthing class. The woman who ran the class had made them repeat together, "Nothing is more important than that little baby. Nothing is more important than that little baby." He harboured secret fears that they might drive off one day with the baby carrier on the top of the car or forget the child in a grocery market or simply sleep in on a lazy Sunday morning, when sleep takes precedence over responsibility. A friend of his had warned that he might drop the baby on its head as he had. "They're tough. They bounce back." That was a horrid thought.

"You've got to get an anesthetist," she said, her eyes glaring. The pain was getting to be too much. He went to the nursing station. No one was there. Down the hall he heard a woman screaming and the nurses telling her to be quiet. She had drawn a crowd. He needed to get anesthetic for his wife. Why were the nurses focused on this one patient and not his wife? When one nurse did emerge from the screamer's room, he ran to her. "Can't you see we're busy now?" was the response that cut him off before he could open his mouth.

"But my wife is in pain. Is that woman having a baby as well?"

"No," said the nurse. "She's a sixteen-year-old having false labour."

"Well," he started to shout, "my wife is in real labour, and she needs an anesthetist."

The nurse paused, sighed, and said, "I will see what I can do."

Hours passed. Midnight came and went. There were no nurses around.

He felt helpless. She felt horrific pain. He went back to the desk. The screaming had stopped. A night nurse had come on her shift. "I am demanding an anesthetist for my wife, right now!"

"Why?" asked the night nurse.

"What do you think?" he shouted back.

"I'll page him now."

A few minutes later the night nurse returned. "Has no one been in to see you? Who is your doctor?" They told the nurse her name. "She's off this weekend. The anesthetist can't get up here because two drunks down in emergency walked in front of a streetcar. He says he'll get up here as soon as he can." The anesthetist arrived at two in the morning.

"You are too far dilated," he said. "I can't give you anything but a local right now. Who is your doctor?" They explained that the doctor had never been in. "That's terrible. I'll get the on-duty in here right now."

A doctor arrived and examined her. A dark look fell upon the physician's face. "I think we're going to have to prep you for a C-section. We can't find a heartbeat, and we're afraid the baby is dead." The couple's eyes met and both felt a terrible despair as the life was torn out of their souls. Through the pain and the fear they wanted to reach out for an instant and hold each other, but the crowd of nurses now in attendance, the anesthetist, and the doctor pushed them farther apart.

On their prenatal tour of the hospital they had been taken into the surgery. It was a cold room with a fluorescent fixture in the ceiling and yellow wall tiles. The look of it initially frightened them both.

She held his hand but turned away and tried to bury her face in a pillow. He looked at his watch and it was three in the morning.

The world was still asleep, and he reminded himself that the rarest form of courage is three-o'clock-in-the-morning courage. He squeezed his wife's hand. "It will be all right. I believe everything will be all right." He wasn't sure himself, but he needed to comfort her. She pulled her hand away and sobbed.

A surgeon came in, followed by the doctor and the anesthetist and two nurses. The surgeon examined her and then spoke, "It is too late to do a C-section. The baby is in the canal and crowning. You'll have to go through with the birth regardless of the outcome. I just want you to be prepared for what will happen." A nurse bent over and ran a stethoscope around the wife's belly. "Doctor! I have a heartbeat!" The doctors, one by one, listened. The tiny sound of life was still there, ticking like an alarm clock in the darkness before dawn. "The child is definitely in distress," the doctor said, "but we'll just have to wait. It won't be long now."

When the group left except for a single nurse, the couple sat in silence. The husband was at a loss for words.

"She will probably be brain damaged," the wife said.

"You don't know that yet," he replied, "but, what is ours is ours, and we will love it and care for it no matter what." He closed his eyes and waited.

A little while later his wife cried out. The nurse who had stayed in the room ran to get the doctors and the other members of the delivery team. A pale, grey, half-living light was radiating through the windows. He watched as their daughter emerged, one eye open, a frightened look on her tiny face. The team immediately pushed him aside, and he stood back as a tangle of stethoscopes and commands blocked his view of the baby and his wife. A nurse turned to him and thrust something into his hands. "Here are the emergency keys to the elevator. Run ahead and commandeer it. We're taking the baby up three floors to the neonatal intensive care ward." He did as she commanded. He rode up with the surgeon and three nurses, but was told he couldn't come in at the door of the ward. He stood helpless. He ran back down the flights of stairs to his wife's floor, but the room was crowded with more medical bodies. "You can't come in," they shouted at him. "We're working to save her. Don't come back for at least two hours." He returned to the upper floors to check on the baby.

At the door he called into the ward. "How is she?"

An answer came from within. "We're working on her. She likely won't live past noon today. Don't tell your wife. She is in equally bad shape." He looked at his watch. It was 7:25 a.m. Time of birth had been 7:13 a.m.

He took the elevator back to his wife's floor. He didn't know what to do. He needed a phone to call his parents. They might know what to do. He wandered up and down the halls. His wife's room was 227. He found a blue room with a strange blue light flooding in the window. An old black rotary phone reposed in the middle of the floor, its heavy black cord running into the wall. He sat down cross-legged and dialed. His mother picked up at the other end.

"Mom, the baby has come, but something went dreadfully wrong. You'd better get down here. The baby won't live past noon ... they are both in distress. They're working on both. I don't know what to do."

He hung up the receiver and sat back on the floor. He got the sense that someone was watching and looked out the window. Instead of the pale blue light, a warmth entered his body, and his neck and shoulders relaxed. Someone was touching him deep inside with a presence that he thought was something close to brilliance, something close to love, bringing a peace within him that he had never felt before; it resembled a breath of warm wind on a summer night when the sky is full of stars and eternity draws a tiny thread from the most distant light and ties it to the heart. He turned and saw a life-size statue of the Virgin Mary in the corner behind him. He hadn't noticed it when he'd come in. She was veiled in blue and her hands were outstretched. He kneeled before the veiled figure with the gentle face.

"Please, Virgin Mother. I'm not a Catholic, but I am in distress. Please help me. I want so much to be a father, and my wife wants so much to be a mother. Our baby is dying. My wife is in trouble. Please help my wife and my little daughter. I don't know what I would do without them. I feel so helpless. I don't know what to do." There was a long silence until he suddenly felt the need to go upstairs and check on his daughter.

In the neonatal intensive care ward, the throng of doctors who had accompanied the baby from the maternity ward downstairs had left. A lone nurse was standing over the incubator. "It is all right to come in and see her. You're the father? I've been doing therapeutic touch on her. They aren't sure whether she will make it. The doctor wants to speak with you. It does not look good for her." The baby's heart monitor was a series of jagged, torn lines moving across the screen. In the room there were other incubators with tiny little grey-skinned dolls in pink or blue toques, all wiggling their arms and struggling for life. He couldn't understand how his large, pink, developed baby was in with these others. A choir of monitors beeped out of sync with each other.

He pulled a stool up to the incubator. "Keep the doors closed," said the nurse.

"But is she going to die?" he asked.

"The truth? Yes, most likely, and before noon." The nurse turned away to attend to another child.

He looked at the child, asleep in the plastic box. This was his daughter, and he wanted this child to grow up and live with them. He wanted to love her all the remaining days of his life and raise her and guide her into the world. He imagined the day of her high school graduation, the morning of her wedding, the times they would spend together as father and daughter. *Damn it*, he thought, *if my child is going to die at least I'll be able to say I sang to her once*. With that he opened one of the round port holes on the side of the box, reached in, and stroked her right hand. The child grasped and held onto his left pinky, and with that he spoke to his newborn daughter as he had every night since the couple learned they were pregnant: "Hello, baby, this is your daddy." He broke into "Somewhere over the Rainbow," and her eyes opened wide and grew wider as she looked directly at him. She recognized the voice and the grip tightened.

With that, the heart suddenly changed. The rhythm became regular, melodic, and constant. Her heart began to sing. The alarm on the monitor went off, and the nurse came running. "What have you done?" she asked.

"I sang to my baby," he replied. "If she's going to die, I wanted to be able to say that I sang to her at least once. That's my obligation as a parent. That's my right."

An elderly doctor, who had been examining a child around the corner, came up to the incubator and stared in disbelief at the monitor. "You sang to her?" he asked. He opened the lid of the container and checked her over. "I was ready to write this child's death certificate," he said. "Now, everything looks fine."

"Don't I know you?" the husband asked.

"I don't know," the physician replied. "My name is Dr. Hanley. I'm retiring today. Your daughter is my last patient. I thought I was going to go out on a losing note, but this baby's heart is as strong as I've seen."

"Dr. Hanley? I think I know you. You had a practice in North Toronto on Lawrence Avenue."

"I did until last week."

"When I was a little boy, I was given up for dead. I had gastroenteritis and had been sent home from the children's hospital to die. You were subbing for my regular doctor. You sat beside my bed the whole night with my parents until you were able to say that I was going to pull through. I had red hair."

"And your room was decorated in ships."

"Yes!"

"I remember you quite well. I'm glad I was here to see this. Your daughter is a miracle baby." The doctor hugged the husband, they shook hands, and he said, "Keep singing." And with that he left, but not before calling over his shoulder, "Have fun with your lovely daughter. She's a fighter and a keeper." A woman in a burka who had been listening to the conversation came running across the room. "Please! Please! Sing to my baby! Sing to my baby!" And with that, he moved to the middle of the ward and belted out the old Harold Arlen standard, not with fear or embarrassment, but with a feeling of great joy.

His parents appeared at the door of the neonatal ward. They came in cautiously as he sung of happy little blue birds flying so high they touched the place where heaven paints its miracles on the ceiling of the world. They looked at him as if he'd lost his mind.

His father waited at the door, tears in his eyes. His mother came forward and looked at the alert child lying in her incubator.

"Oh, she is beautiful. She is so beautiful. She's perfect. She's a miracle."

"And Mom, she's going to live. She's going to be fine."

Seven years and ten months later, the husband and wife and their daughter went out into the darkness of a northern night to lie together on a dock and look up at the stars and falling Perseids and share a bag of marshmallows. The gentle ripples of the calmed, still bay softly lapped at the moorings but soon vanished into silence as the world fell away beneath them. Meteors were shooting from the heavens, lighting up the sky in miraculous moments of brilliance, and the Milky Way spread across the endless breadth of night. The child slipped her warm hand into his, and he shuffled his free hand along the deck until he found his wife's and squeezed it. The three held hands and looked on in wonder with nothing between them and eternity.

"There are so many stars," the little girl said. "I had no idea there were so many. Did I come from out there somewhere?"

"Maybe," said his wife. "Blessings come from heaven."

There was a long silence.

"And Dadda?"

"Yes, pumpkin?"

"The universe is full of miracles. It is just like us."

When in a Fine Day's Running

We have a child now, our son. I was late marrying. This is a difficult city in which to meet one's mate. You can look everywhere, but the woman you dream about doesn't exactly jump out at you. You want a woman who reminds you of the women you once knew. They were beautiful and whole and warm.

Luckily, though, I did meet someone. She is as close to my dream as I can imagine. I think her last name is Lander. She came from some place far away. She is one of those people who always knows how to help. I don't know what she saw in me, but she was everything I wanted. And I hadn't wanted anything in my life before I met her.

We married, and for the first time I saw my body and hers together, without clothes, as if we were … the word she used for it was *vulnerable*. Everyone is vulnerable. We are warm when we are together. I feel something melting deep within me. I think it must be *beauty*.

I watched with awe as she grew rounder and fuller with each day. The pregnancy, like most pregnancies I have heard about, was fraught with fear. Fear of complications, fear of a child being stillborn, fear of handicaps—those things haunt what should be one of the most beautiful times in a couple's life together. In this case, the fears were all unfounded.

I watch our child with wonder. The beauty of having a child is that you get to admire a bit of yourself in that small person. I look at him, and I see how I might have been myself had I been permitted to be myself, yet different. You have the opportunity to find that little bit of your lost years in the way a child plays with crayons or scribbles letters in the snow, pretending that they have something significant to say. I remember meeting an old man as he snowshoed across the open land one day. He said he had been an anatomy professor once upon a time. I asked him what he meant by that, and he said he'd studied life.

"You must have had to look hard," I replied.

"Not in those days," he said smiling. "Life always finds a way. Even today." We both stared at my son who was learning to use the snowshoes I had made for him out of some old metal and some coyote gutting. He moved quickly, cutting his way through the grey shadow of the afternoon.

When I was four, I looked up at a very orange sky after dinner one night. It glowed. The stars seemed shadows by comparison. I asked my father why it stayed that colour long after sunset.

"They're testing hydrogen bombs in the US. They exploded one last week in Wyoming, and they're going to be testing in the Atlantic next week."

"Will I be able to hear the bombs, Daddy?"

"No. But the sky will be pumpkin for some time to come," he said and cleared his throat to end the conversation. I lived inside a pumpkin. I could grow up to be a ghost.

My first weeks in kindergarten in the autumn of 1962 were a

strange adjustment for me. I presented my hand to my teacher and introduced myself formally as I had been taught at nursery school. She told me to sit down and shut up. The other children were running wild. The teacher had a bell on her desk like the ones I'd seen in hotel lobbies. Ring. Ring. Everyone stopped what they were doing. "Tidy up time," she announced.

We were putting our play things away. I hadn't played. I'd simply put my hands in my pockets and went around trying to make conversation with anyone who would respond. No one responded.

A little while later, we were seated at our tiny oak desks. There was a small trench at the edge of the desktop. I didn't know what it was for, but I imagined my toy soldiers hunkered down in that hollow, shooting at the enemy. That is when the teacher screamed, "Duck and cover!"

We dropped what we were doing and crouched beneath the desks, our heads in our knees as we had been taught, and our hands clasping the square, oak front legs that were thicker than our own.

"Not quick enough," the teacher hollered as she marched up and down the rows. "Not quick enough." She reached beneath the desk and pulled me out by the scruff of my short hair. "You didn't pull your chair in after you for protection! You are dead! Go stand in the corner!" I stood there, a ghost. Away from the others, I felt as if I had survived something they would not. Ghosts don't die because they are already dead.

We were told that "The Bomb" might fall at any time. One boy said "neato" at the prospect. I had seen an article about the bomb in a copy of *Life* magazine in my pediatrician's office and had asked my mother to explain it to me.

"That won't happen here," she reassured me as I stared at an outdated picture of two bald men (presumably Eisenhower and Khrushchev at the Vienna Conference of 1958).

The Cold War came to my school a month later, in mid-October, 1962. My mother, who had been rocking my sister in her arms all morning, watched the television with me as various reporters talked about the reconnaissance pictures of the missiles in Cuba and showed photographs of Russian freighters steaming across the Atlantic.

When I arrived at school after lunch, the teacher sat in the corner in an eerie silence. She was staring into space and holding a picture of her late husband. The pandemonium of forty five-year-olds erupted all around her. The bell sounded and she didn't play the chords on the piano that usually snapped us into circle time. Instead the principal appeared at the door and summoned her. They conversed quietly and several times turned and glanced at us. He disappeared down the dark corridor, and I never saw him again. The teacher turned and shouted, "Everyone line up. We are going downstairs!" The school I went to was a single-story structure, and I had no idea there was a basement. It sounded like a good adventure.

We filed into the building's nether regions, to a boiler room which was nothing more than a large space with a cement floor and some janitor's equipment leaned against the wall in the far corner. The order was to sit on the floor in the tuck position we took when we were commanded to duck and cover beneath our desks.

I looked up through the barred window and saw the shadows and silhouettes of the boys and girls from the older grades running from the school. The grade threes were sandwiched together over by the janitor's bench in the dark corner. Next to them were the grade twos and the grade ones. My class was closest to the stairwell. The teachers walked up and down around the periphery of our huddled figures. Suddenly, one of the second-grade teachers began to cry. Her crying set off some of the girls and a few of the boys in her class. Then the other teachers began to cry. Someone raised a hand and asked, "Why are we crying?" and a male teacher turned on us like an angry dog and screamed, "Shut up! The world is going to blow up!" This admission set the entire basement off into a biblical wail. I thought the whole thing was stupid.

I was sitting next to the exit door and could see daylight at the top of the staircase. I had had as much as I could take. As the teachers rushed *en masse* to a second grader who was throwing up all over her classmates, I stood up, straightened my trousers, and walked up the stairs to the outside door. It was a beautiful, clear though cool October afternoon. The sun was shining, and the schoolyard was fringed with the last stalks of goldenrod. It was too beautiful a day for the world to blow up, and besides, my grandmother had taught me a prayer that concluded with the words "world without end, Amen." I said the word *Amen* under my breath and set off for home.

I rang the bell at our front door. My mother opened the inner door but not the glass storm door my father installed for winter.

"What are you doing home and without your jacket?"

"Is the world going to blow up?" I asked her.

She undid the latch on the outer door. "I don't know," she said, "but c'mon in, and we'll watch it on TV."

A few minutes later, there was a frantic call from the school to inform my mother, "Your son is missing, and at a terrible time of crisis." My mother's voice sounded muffled from the hall, though I could sense the anger and strain in her words. We sat together until dinnertime.

I watched the Cuban missile crisis unfold. It was an education. In mid-afternoon, President Kennedy appeared and moved through a crowd of congressmen. All the while, my mother explained the structure and workings of the US government, the sides in the Cold War and what they were arguing about, and why Canada would not be bombed. Only later did I learn that a Toronto newspaper had, the night before, run a front-page story titled "What If the Bomb Fell at Avenue Road and Bloor?" and that many people assumed that the bomb was going to fall at Avenue Road and Bloor and tried to flee north to their cottages, where they believed they would be safe. The Russians would not waste a bomb on a cottage.

Highway 400 northbound was jammed with panicky people. Cars broke down or ran out of gas. There was footage on the *CBC Evening News* of a woman, screaming and crying, running with a baby in her arms. There was a look of terror in her eyes. She was going to run to her cottage. My mother and I spent the early evening talking about what was happening as I ate my dinner in front of the television set. When she turned it off at my bed time, the screen flashed a single bright, distant light that gradually faded to nothing. I wish I knew what that light reminds me of.

History, or what I know of it now, says that on an October Tuesday when I was five, the Russians did not turn back their missile boats in time for supper, as we'd hoped. I have always lived with the uneasy feeling that history was different someplace else, and that the place where I am now is a no-place that was created out of a single nightmare from which I could not wake. I heard my father say something like that about history once.

In my recurring dream, I see a young president staring at a wall of photographs of ships. Their wakes trail behind them, and the sea around them is rippled like the skin of an elephant. He has his hand tucked under his chin. He turns to his Secretary of State, an odd-looking man with slicked-back hair, who has taken off his glasses momentarily because the fatigue of stress has built up behind his eyes. The President points to the pictures and to a map where a junior officer has just posted tiny red missiles along the Iron Curtain. "This is a new type of language," says Kennedy. "And I am going to learn to speak it." And at that point I always wake up. I feel the cold in the room around me. I look out the window at the sky that is always black as black at night, and I remember a strange song about wishing on something that lies hidden behind the clouds. The ships, as far as I know, sailed on to Havana and launched their rockets at the cities of North America. The Americans and their allies pointed their weapons at the Soviets. School was cancelled the next morning. In place of Captain Kangaroo, President Kennedy wept, his head not thrown back the way it usually was when he spoke, but tilted slightly down like a man defeated, his voice soft and low and full of disappointment. "Nothing can convince us of the importance of humanity more than facing the end of it, and nothing is more apparent than that we have reached our last best vision of ourselves."

My parents took me into the fruit cellar beneath the front porch. My elderly grandparents huddled with us in the darkness, and I fell asleep. When I woke, my mother was bleeding from the ears and my father was weeping. My baby sister was limp in my mother's arms, and when I stood up to kiss her awake as I often did early in the morning, I saw that the side of her face was blistered. She had been closest to the tiny air vent in the cellar. I had been kept warm beneath my grandmother. My grandfather sat in the corner—we were all illumined briefly by candlelight, and my father said we would have to save what light we could for later. My grandfather's eyes were wide open with a look of dismay written on his face. He held my grandmother, who had collapsed in his arms, and refused to let her go. We were all white, and the concrete ceiling seemed ajar. Then my father blew out the light.

I grew up in darkness. When the light returned, a faint light like the faint hope my father often spoke of, my clothes were way too small, and my arms and legs protruded from the fraying cloth like the shoots of flowers that used to come up in our garden when the snow vanished. Only now, the snow never left us. Ill as he was, my father took the time to teach me how to read. I found the ruins of the local library, and what had not been consumed by flames after the blast was a small school for me. Of my old school, nothing remained. I stared into the pit. The bricks had been removed to make new shelters. A few pieces of the small oak desks lay broken on the basketball court, but most had either been destroyed in the explosion or taken for firewood. I don't know who thought those puny things would protect us.

The snow fell and fell and eventually filled in the landscape, turning fire hydrants and cars to anomalous roundings in the snow. Eventually, through the years of endless blizzards and constant Februaries, the snow reached to where our second story had been.

I have the snow to thank for my survival. Animals, especially hungry animals, have to stay on the surface. Finished with the initial clawing and scratching at the bodies, the animals became vicious, and viciousness makes creatures careless. They came to us if we waited long enough. The snow also froze the bodies, so disease did not spread, and by the time the world of the past had been covered over, it seemed as if a page in time had been rubbed clean with an eraser.

The neighbourhood as I had known it did not exist. We thought the Pilkingtons down the block might have gotten through. He had been called a paranoid nutcase by just about everyone on the street, but we were sure his shelter at the back of his garden had survived the blast. One day I went down to where their house had stood with a shovel and began to dig, just for the fun of it. The blade clanged on the top of the shelter. But when I looked closer, I saw the roof had fallen in. Mr. and Mrs. Pilkington and their dog Yahtzee sat against a wall, their faces shrivelled to a wince and their eyes staring ahead into the darkness of the future.

Not long after that, the helicopters started to arrive. I was the fastest in snowshoes and got to them first. That package, as cumbersome as it was to drag back across the snow with one hand—I had a pitchfork in the other and swung it at anyone who came close—kept my father and I alive for a little over a year. A woman pleaded with me to share some with her. She said she had a baby to feed. But then the crust of snow gave way beneath her, and all I heard was her cry for help as she drowned beneath the white. Now that I am a father, I regret not helping her that day, but I had to make a choice. Survival is all about choices, and you only choose to help the ones you love. I thought about things like that to pass the time. Time in the land of endless snow doesn't mean much. In fact, a person doesn't want to keep track of time at all. A day? A night? It doesn't matter. They all pass. Each one is a test of survival, and my survival was like anyone else's survival. There were moments of despair, but when despair becomes the norm a person just gets used to it. There were moments of happiness, too. I laughed, though maybe nothing was funny at all. Despair also makes a person laugh.

I laughed and laughed and fell down in the snow when the helicopters finally landed. The first landers were explorers from the other side of the world—from places that had not received a bomb on that day in 1962. They said, "Do you know what year it is?" I shook my head.

They asked, "Do you know your name?" I hadn't used it in years.

"I think it is Son. My father called me that." There had been a boy down the block who was younger than me. His parents didn't make it home in time to be with him. He didn't last long. I saw his body being hauled off by some coyotes I could not catch and kill for food. We always called him "Bub." I knew that Bub was not my name.

The second party of landers came several weeks later. That is when the anatomy professor strolled into the neighbourhood and became a fixture for several years. He started walking one day in search of his own death, and he could not find it. He was the one who said, "Life will always find a way." At first I didn't believe him. "You don't realize it, but we're all long shots. We're all here because in some way—when we were conceived, when we were infants, when we encountered the great hardship, we all beat the odds. We're all long shots. If you're a betting man, you gotta love it." Life did find a way, at least for me. That was when I met my wife. She sat me down to cut my hair and shave my beard. I hadn't felt the cool of air on my skin or had a warm meal for as far back as I could remember. She asked my name and laughed when I pointed to myself and said, "Son. Here." I mumbled a lot for a long time before I became, in her words, "conversant."

I don't know what makes people fall in love. I don't know why someone would fall in love with someone who has nothing and be willing to remain with them in a land of nothing. I told her, "Why not be pioneers in a world that was finally beginning to show signs of life?" We weren't permitted to leave. They could come among us, but we could not go among them. My wife could foresee what was coming. My world was gradually being reborn. I loved the way snowflakes settled in her soft brown hair. I held the strands between my fingers and watched as the falling melted against my breath. "That is what we mean by springtime," she said softly.

I tell my son the world used to be a very different place.

"How different?" he asks.

"Well, you've never been able to do something called running because the snow is still too deep." The snow had been melting slowly for over a year, and I heard streams of water chattering beneath the ice as if they were tunnelling to find a way out.

"What's running, Dad?" he questions.

"It is when you pick up your legs, and they move so quickly beneath you that you reach the other side of the world and stare at the sun rising over the ocean on a summer morning as the first rays chase tiny lights from the sky and the world fills with colours. Remember I told you about the sun behind the clouds and the reason we have days? Well, when there is no snow, you can run."

"You can't do that," he shakes his head.

"But you can, you can, when in a fine day's running you have no limits and no one holds you back, because the world and everything in it is limitless. Your feet can carry you anywhere. It is the same feeling you have when you find someone you can love with all your heart. And your heart, just like your feet, can't stop moving. That's the way your mother makes me feel. That's the way you make me feel."

My wife turns to me in the night and touches my arm with the warmth of her hand though she doesn't realize it. She is sleeping through history just like me. And when I am awakened by something in me that won't go away, I realize it is a dream I must keep dreaming because life is a nightmare.

And I love the dream. My parents and grandparents are with me. There is green all over the ground, not just in the smocks and mittens the relief workers bring us from the other side of the world, but real green, green I can smell. I want to bend down and taste it and eat it and feel it inside me, moving like the warmth of my wife or the sound of water running beneath the snow. And in the dream I am watching my baby sister. She is alive and grown up, and she is speaking to a room full of people, and I am so proud of her. I am the first to my feet when she finishes her speech, and the audience applauds and understands that what she has said is new and real and green.

Author Biography

Bruce Meyer is the award-winning author of forty-five books of poetry, short fiction, non-fiction, and literary journalism. His most recent books include the poetry collections *A Book of Bread* (2012), *The Obsession Book of Timbuktu* (2014), *Testing the Elements* (2014), *The Seasons* (2014), which won an IPPY Medal from the American Association of Independent Publishers and was short-listed for the Indie-Fab Award for the best book of poems published in North America by the Independent Booksellers Association of America, and the forthcoming *The Arrow of Time* (2015). With Barry Callaghan he published the ground-breaking anthology *We Wasn't Pals: Canadian Poetry and Prose of the First World War* (2000, 2014 with an afterword by Margaret Atwood). His spoken word work includes the CBC's bestselling CD series, *The Great Books and Great Poetry.* His non-fiction volume *The Golden Thread: A Reader's Journey Through the Great Books* was a national bestseller in 2000. He was the inaugural Poet Laureate of the City of Barrie and is professor of Creative Writing and Communications at Georgian College and Visiting Professor of Literature at Victoria College in the University of Toronto. He lives in Barrie, Ontario.

Author Acknowledgements

I would like to say a very special thank you to my editor, Deanna Janovski, whose brilliant editorial work did much to improve these stories and who taught me a great deal about precision in fiction. Thank you to Heather Wood for her energies in spreading the word about this book; to Molly Peacock of Toronto, who suggested that "A Chronicle of Magpies" should be evolved into a novella; to Barry Callaghan who showed me that less is more in a short story; to Leon Rooke, Anne Michaels, and Lauren Carter for their preliminary thoughts on the manuscript; to Andrew Pyper and Ania Szado for their enthusiasm and gracious support; to Paul Romero of Bryant Park, New York, David Bigham of Mount Forest, and Linda Laforge of Barrie for being great sounding boards for these stories; to Dora Goh of the Ontario Multicultural Society for her assistance with the research for "The Dragon Cloth;" to Karen Wetmore and the staff of Grenville Printing at Georgian College for their great services as the manuscript developed; to Earlene Angevine of Manitoulin Island and Kent Smith of Barrie and Muskoka for providing me with quiet places to write when I needed them; and to my colleagues and students at Georgian College in Barrie and Victoria College at the University of Toronto. A very special thank you to Halli Villegas who chose this book for publication and who encouraged me to tell these stories, and to Jim Nason of Tightrope Books for his support and belief in seeing this project through to its conclusion. And to Kerry, Katie, Margaret, and Carolyn for the stories they have told me and their love of telling them.